Sweeney's Ghost

Sweeney's Ghost

written and illustrated by
LEONARD EVERETT FISHER

Doubleday & Company, Inc., Garden City, New York
1975

38088

Library of Congress Cataloging in Publication Data

Fisher, Leonard Everett.
  Sweeney's ghost.

  SUMMARY: A vacationing family discover their rented Jamaican
villa is haunted by the ghost of a pirate.
  [1. Ghost stories. 2. Jamaica—Fiction] I. Title.
PZ7.F533Sw   [Fic]
ISBN 0-385-08800-0 Trade
      0-385-08655-5 Prebound
Library of Congress Catalog Card Number 73–9027

For Marge,

Julie, Susan and James

CONTENTS

SATURDAY
February 19, 1972

The 747 came out of the Cuban sky gracefully arcing south-westward across the sparkling Caribbean. Slowly the great airplane straightened out its flight path and rapidly descended. A minute or two later, the huge, gleaming white, blue-striped jet, its braking engines whining in reverse, roared down the incoming runway of Jamaica's International Airport at Montego Bay—Mo Bay for short.

"Now arriving from New York," the airport's loudspeaker system gravely intoned, "Pan American Flight 221—Pan American—Flight 221—from New York, JFK."

To the uninitiated "JFK" simply indicated John Fitzgerald

1

Kennedy International Airport. A few more bits of information drifted from the speakers and echoed overhead. No one understood a single word of it. The hollow syllables were garbled and overwhelmed by the shattering, ear-splitting noise of a nearby Air Jamaica jet preparing to depart for JFK, New York.

The incoming 747—the world's largest commercial aircraft —looking more like a gigantic white porpoise with two wings and a misplaced fin, taxied about in the brilliant early afternoon sunshine heading for the terminal building. Finally, it came to rest a few yards from the building's "Arrivals" section.

Inside the spacious aircraft, a dozen cheerfully exhausted stewardesses had already stowed the dirty luncheon trays, hundreds of plastic knives, forks, spoons, cups, and swizzle sticks—not to mention magazines, pillows, and miscellaneous garbage.

"Please have your necessary documents ready for Jamaica health, customs, and immigration officials," they were now telling their three hundred or more passengers. "We trust you have had a pleasant flight and hope you enjoy your stay here in Jamaica. Thank you for flying Pan American."

And that was that!

Nearly everyone began to stand and peer through the windows with sunny expectations. There was the usual quiet commotion as tangled, seemingly disembodied, arms and hands reached for clothing bags, carry-on luggage, tennis racquets, and what not. The vacationing Framers—Lester, Mildred and children: Jennifer, Sarilee, and Jojo—had some

2

of each of these including a Bloomingdale's shopping bag full of skin-diving gear. None of this equipment—masks, fins, and snorkels—would fit into their already jammed luggage, so—a Bloomingdale's shopping bag.

Little by little, knots of impatient travelers began shuffling and slithering toward the still sealed exit, pressing and squeezing the five Framers before them like a giant caterpillar, the kind one might see on a TV horror science fiction movie. The Framers seemed to grow smaller as the human caterpillar, swaying and undulating, grew larger. All the while a never-ending recording of soft, romantic music wafted through their economy-class compartment as if to keep the restless caterpillar calm and friendly while it waited to disembark.

At least half of the economy-class voyagers were Connecticut school kids and their parents. The Framers were part of this legion, living and paying their taxes in Aspetuck, a small town north of the Merritt Parkway and about forty miles from New York City. Actually, only the Framer children were authentic Connecticut Yankees, all having been born in Norwalk Hospital. But not Les and Millie. They were transplanted Manhattanites who departed the great city in the late '50s during the massive emigration to the suburbs.

At any rate, yesterday, Friday, the eight school weeks following the Christmas recess had come to an end. Accordingly, public education in the state of Connecticut was now entitled to a rest. By tacking the two weekends on to both ends of the five-day school week bonus, the whole thing became a glorious nine-day February holiday. And in affluent Fairfield County—or at least a good portion of

3

southern Connecticut—this triggered an exodus from New York's JFK airport that was not unlike a well-orchestrated flight of southbound migratory birds.

The pale winter-garbed passengers on Flight 221 were more than ready to forget the snow and ice that was paralyzing New York and New England—now three and a half hours behind them. At precisely 1:10 P.M., the time promised in the airline schedule, surprisingly enough—a promise often difficult to keep for one reason or another—the exit door was swung open. Out of the air-conditioned musical airplane and into the clinging heat of the West Indian sun stumbled the Framers followed by the eager horde, all gasping, momentarily staggered by the sudden change in climate.

Lester Framer, nearing fifty and a bit overweight, was an inveterate traveler. His mobility began years ago when he enlisted in the Army during World War II to fight Germans but ended up fighting the Japanese, one Pacific island at a time. His current career as an executive for a firm that produced and distributed plastic handle-bar tape for 10-speed bicycles and other plastic sporting goods like Badminton shuttlecocks, took him all over the United States. He could not even remember how many times he had been to Hong Kong, the site of his company's factory. Only once had he been to Italy to call on Italian bike manufacturers. The rest of the time he spent on the Penn Central Railroad commuting between his home in Aspetuck and his New York office. The trouble was that Les's entire traveling outlook was colored by his New York commuting. He liked to be in new places but he hated the idea of getting there.

Millie, his tireless wife, was just the opposite. A non-job-holding mother, devoted to her husband, children, and home but enslaved by them all, she continuously looked forward to traveling—to getting away. So accustomed was Millie Framer to her everyday routine that she hated to be in new places enjoying only the excitement of getting there. To Les, traveling was arriving somewhere without having moved. To Millie, traveling was moving somewhere without arriving.

As overweight as Les was, that is how underweight Millie was. Tall, thin, and very angular, she blamed it all in recent months on the eternal oppression of women.

"Women's Lib is for me," she cried out one day last year. She hoisted her colors for the Cause, turning what little undivided attention she had left of her Aspetuck day toward Little League baseball. Millie became obsessed with the idea that there should be a Little League for girls; and that a championship girls team should play a championship boys team in the Williamsport, Pennsylvania, Little League World Series. During the spring of last year a group of women led by Millie picketed the Little League games in Aspetuck and bombarded the local newspapers with protest letters. For her part, Millie, the president of G.A.A.L.L.S. (Girls All-American Little League Society), planned to use her Jamaica vacation to plot new strategy for the upcoming season.

The Framer kids, on the other hand, were obsessed by different things. Jennifer, aloof, lanky, coolly attractive was incorruptible. If boys interested her she did not show it. What seemed to surface mostly was a practiced contempt. At sixteen going on seventeen, Jennifer could throw a better pass than the star quarterback on the high school football team. She could hit towering fly balls on demand and given half a chance she could play third base better than any boy within fifty miles of Aspetuck. Not only that, she held every girl's track record in interscholastic state-wide competition with meet times that equalled and sometimes bettered the best of the boys. Jennifer, in brief, was the apple of her mother's eye. She was the one offspring who would inherit the fruits of her mother's labors with G.A.A.L.L.S. She would be the first woman to play with a major league club as a star third baseman—that would have to be changed to baseperson, of course.

Sarilee, fourteen, was not yet as tall as her sister but all legs just the same, an indication that she would arrive someday at a similar lanky attractiveness. But that is where the similarity ended. Unlike her cool sister, Sarilee was a stormy soul when not engaged in her full-time activity of chasing boys. The fact was that Sarilee was only a nickname, something stately Jennifer would never permit. Her real name was Suzette, a legal fixture she detested from an early age.

One day Les picked up sixth-grader Suzette at school. Spying her in a crowd of friends, he called to her, "Suzette! Over here! Suzette!" Suzette leaped at her father, screaming, "Don't you ever call me that again, ever!"

"Well, O.K., Cupcake. Never again!"

6

"Cupcake!" someone chortled at Les's startled response.

"How about coffeecake?"

"Sara Lee. That's it. Sara Lee. A great name in cakes!"

That was it. Sara Lee. The name stuck. And with a more independent spelling it became Sarilee much to Suzette's unaccountable amusement.

Brother Jojo, twelve, wasn't Jojo either. His name was Jonathan. It seems that when he was an infant, a relative presented him with a sterling silver monogrammed yoyo. Jonathan could not even talk yet, let alone maneuver the fancy toy. Finally the day came.

Jonathan gurgled and spoke his first words. Not ma-ma or da-da like most babies, but jo-jo. Then he burst into tears which were magically transformed into smiles when Les gave him his yoyo.

"How about that?" beamed his adoring father. "My boy can talk!" And from that day to this Jonathan Framer has been Jojo Framer to the world.

But Jojo belied his nickname. He was a bright, level-headed, studious young man more interested in electro-magnetic waves and ultrasonics than he was in girls. He could not spell, he could not add and he was a terrible athlete. But ask him what the "Doppler effect" was and his reply would be so lucid, so expert as to be positively awesome. Jojo liked to read a great deal but not necessarily what he could find in the school library. During the past year, Jojo temporarily lost interest in electromagnetic waves and ultrasonics, frustrated over the fact that his parents refused to provide him with a complete laboratory such as those at the Massachusetts Institute of Technology.

"Don't worry," Jojo warned his parents, "I'll find the money."

With that and knowing he would soon be in Jamaica, Jojo Framer turned his mind in a more sinister direction. He began to look into piracy on the high seas, the rabble of seafaring cutthroats that stalked the Spanish Main so long ago and the treasure they left behind. To Jojo, now steeped in the lore and history of Caribbean pirates, going to Jamaica, their ancient stronghold, was like a homecoming.

In a looser sense it was a homecoming for all the Framers. Three years before, Les, Millie, and the kids had come to the island on just such a February jaunt as this one. They had rented a small, inexpensive house with a swimming pool about twenty-five miles east of Mo Bay in Trelawny Parish. The house was part of an eight-day package deal that included a cook, maid, gardener, and watchman. All they had to do was rent a car and buy their own food at the local markets in nearby Falmouth, the latter being a colorful, educational, and entertaining experience. The former was a different kind of adventure.

It took Les all of eight days, if ever, to accustom himself to the right-hand drive car and the Jamaica traffic system—driving on the left-hand side of the road—the wrong side in Les's estimation. Millie refused to drive.

"I produce life," Millie declared with every womanly instinct. "I do not take it away! You drive!"

Millie kept her eyes half shut most of the time, particularly when a mammoth gasoline truck bound for Mo Bay barreled down the narrow coastal highway straddling the center line, if there was a center line. Les sat on the horn and rode the brakes and somehow avoided catastrophe after catastrophe. The kids couldn't care less. They knew that they were destined to live forever, each in his own way. Jennifer and Sarilee sat back and enjoyed the scenery, fascinated by the endless parade of black people whose island they chose to visit, and appalled by the colorful poverty that dotted the winding road. While Jojo carefully noted variations in the Doppler effect with every passing horn-blasting truck.

In any event, the Framers did relax and so thoroughly enjoyed themselves that they vowed to return again.

Now they were back, happily shuffling toward the terminal building with another eight-day package deal.

It was nearly 6:30 P.M. when the overheated Framers' rented car rattled down a potholed road and confronted Limeshade Villa—their vacation home.

The house stood behind a thick cement block wall, alone and dark, on a desolate, scruffy spot. The night was coming fast. None of the surroundings, let alone the house, seemed distinct to the bleary-eyed family. In another half hour or so, the silhouettes would be complete and sharp against the twilight sky. At the moment the sight was diffused in the changing light and atmosphere.

Les let the car engine idle, stopping just short of the driveway entrance, unwilling to proceed farther. None of the Framers imagined that the two-hour drive from Mo Bay would lead to this seemingly bleak place. They had driven the fifty miles eastward along the hotel-strewn north coast, past Ocho Rios, anticipating nothing but a tropical paradise.

"Get a load of this place," moaned Les. "It doesn't look at all like the pictures we saw. Where's the cook, where's the maid, where's the caretaker, and where are all the palm trees?"

"There are a few of them over there," offered Sarilee, pointing to the end of the road some one hundred yards to their right.

10

"Maybe we're in the wrong place," Jojo added.

"No, this is it." Millie sighed, apparently disappointed not so much with the baldness of the area as she was with finally having arrived someplace—anyplace. "This is Sea Turtle Lane, isn't it? That sign says LIMESHADE VILLA, doesn't it? We're here all right. Les, honey, if you put this heap in gear and drive up that driveway past that wall, maybe things will look up."

Les shifted from neutral to first, turned into the driveway and slowly creeped forward until he reached the carport where he shut off the motor.

"It would have been more ideal," he muttered, "if we had arrived sooner while the sun was still reasonably high in the sky."

"Well! Who's fault is that?" Sarilee snarled. "You know, Daddy, we could have been here hours ago if you hadn't hung us up at the airport. What a rip off!"

Les said nothing in his own defense. And except for Jennifer's barb, "First out, last in"—an obvious reference to first, the airplane and secondly, the country of Jamaica—no one else said anything either.

A series of events had unfolded at the terminal building that tried Les's patience, turned him slightly paranoid, and in the end thoroughly chastened him. The Framers had quickly claimed all of their luggage except one unaccountably missing piece. It eventually showed up after nearly all of their co-travelers had left the airport. Les fumed at the baggage handlers. During this unendurable wait, Les drank more free rum punches—courtesy of the Jamaica Tourist Board—than he should have. At one point he sarcastically reminded a nearby policeman that the terminal building should have been air-conditioned by now. The officer politely apologized for the inconvenience. But Les kept reminding him nevertheless. Excusing himself with a respectful salute and a toothy grin that looked like a quarter moon set into his big black face, the policeman casually walked over to the customs table where he had a few words with one of the uniformed inspectors.

In due time, the Framers collected all of their luggage and presented the pile for customs inspection. Instead of the routine examination—perhaps one bag opened, lightly explored, and closed—the Framers were subjected to an intense search. All five pieces of their luggage were opened and minutely examined. Their carry-on Pan Am tote bags were explored. Millie had to empty her large satchel-like shoulder bag. So did the girls. Not even the undersea contents of the Bloomingdale's shopping bag were overlooked. The camera covers were inspected as well as the tennis racquets. In fact, a sealed can of fresh tennis balls was opened, the balls removed and vigorously shaken for any contraband hidden inside.

"What are you looking for?" Les pleaded.

"Weapons, narcotics, and booze, sir," came the smiling polite reply.

"In a tennis ball?"

By the time the customs inspection was over, the luggage hastily restuffed, and the Framers approvingly passed through the next obstacle—Jamaica Immigration—there were no car rentals left. Another exasperating wait. But Les kept quiet. He made no more remarks about the inconvenience, saving them all any further unnecessary grief. A car soon appeared. It was 4:25 P.M. when they finally drove off—on the wrong side of the road.

"I'm hungry," Jojo announced.

"I'm thirsty," said his father.

"We are all thirsty and starving," Millie retorted.

"O.K., O.K., I'll see what's what," Les offered. "Everyone sit tight while I have a quick look around."

No one moved.

"If the place is shut down and the cupboard is bare, we'll head for the Tower Isle dining room. It's only about a mile back down the road. We passed it on the way here."

"That's a fine idea. Let's go there first."

Les did not hear the last remark. He was already at the front door tentatively turning the knob, positive the place was closed and that they would be off for a luxurious dinner at the Tower Isle Hotel. But the door gave willingly, in-

vitingly, and swung open to reveal in the dim light a table, some chairs, and a pair of louvered doors behind them.

"The door is open," Les reported.

"Really?" someone shot back, probably Sarilee.

Les stuck his head inside the entryway and almost fell over trying to keep the rest of him outside.

"Hello! Anyone home?" No one answered. He tried again. "Anyone here?" Still no answer.

"No one's here," he reported.

"That figures," Jojo commented.

"Would you like me to come with you, Daddy?" Jennifer was growing impatient.

Les took a few halting steps into the house encouraged by Millie's challenging scowl and Jennifer's contemptuous reference to his manly courage.

"No need to. No need to. I'll check around." Les finally disappeared into the house. He emerged again a few minutes later after having turned on every light he could find.

"Hey! It's not so bad," he exclaimed. "It seems that we have been expected. Maybe the cook or somebody went looking for us, considering how late we are. There's stuff and ice in the refrig and some packaged goodies and food on the kitchen counter. The stove works. The beds have been turned down. There's even a bar with a couple of stools,

16

running water and the bottled makings for some liquid refreshments. Of course we'll have to shop sometime. But we've got enough to make the rest of the night comfy cozy."

"Beautiful," they all chorused.

"Oh yes, one more thing. How could I forget. The pool is out back. A good size one too. And the underwater lights are on. Anyone care for a swim?"

With that, Millie, Jennifer, Sarilee, and Jojo tumbled out of the car and began lugging baggage into the house. The night was upon them. It had been an exhausting day. And they were all quite happy to have arrived at last—even Millie.

SUNDAY
February 20, 1972

A brief morning rain had left a steamy haze all around. The damp blur was nearly gone now, slowly dissolved by the warming sun. Sunday's bright promise was everywhere.

The sizzle and crackle that came from the kitchen like so many firecrackers on a Chinese New Year, pushed an aroma of bacon and eggs and Jamaican Blue Mountain coffee—all of this laced with the faint fragrances of oranges, limes, pineapple, fresh bread—to every corner of the house. Coraleen Morgan, the Framers' young package-deal-cook-housekeeper, was busy organizing a sumptuous breakfast for the family that arrived too late yesterday for her to meet and who had yet to appear this morning.

19

Coraleen had been at Limeshade until 5:30 P.M. yesterday afternoon. Ordinarily, her day began at 7:00 A.M. and ended at 7:00 P.M. But not yesterday. Martin Martin, the old caretaker-gardener, had left early astride his burro, George, for a night on the town in Ocho Rios. Coraleen, not wanting to be left alone and fearing that the Framers were hopelessly lost or not coming at all, cut her day short. She left no note of any kind and walked a couple of miles farther east toward Oracabessa and home.

This morning she arrived on schedule at seven, crisp and pretty in a shocking pink skirt and a bright, lemon yellow silk blouse imprinted with gold sea gulls. There were spotless white loafers on her feet and a green turban tightly tied around her head. She clutched a pineapple, a net-like bag of oranges, and an Air Jamaica flight bag. The blackness of her skin was so deep and the colors she chose to wear so vibrant that Coraleen Morgan was an abstract painting come to life as well as a warm, animate human being.

No sooner had Coraleen arrived, she removed her shoes, the only pair she owned, and hid them away in the flight bag. The young Jamaican was determined to make them last forever by not wearing them during her work day. In any event, she opened the louver doors that led from the dining area to the patio out back, let in the morning light, a view of the swimming pool and the lush tropical garden dominated by lime trees. Also, sprinkled among the lime trees were a few coconut palms, wild banana trees, breadfruit, grapefruit, almond and pimiento trees, and several hot pepper bushes.

Martin Martin had materialized out of nowhere, delivered the fresh bread to the kitchen door and was vacuuming the pool when Coraleen flung open the doors. For one suspended moment, the scene was a picture postcard upon which remained to be scribbled, "Having a wonderful time, wish you were here."

Behind its seemingly forbidding cement block walls, and unlike its pebbly, lonely environs, Limeshade Villa was an oasis of tropical splendor, well manicured and solidly built.

The house itself was not palatial. Its lack-luster location easily made it one of the cheaper rentals on the otherwise fashionable north coast. One of the more interesting aspects of the house was its shape—a "V"—considered by some to be a radical Jamaican innovation when it was introduced on this spot fifteen years before. Limeshade Villa's white stucco walls and swooping, wide overhanging brown shingled roof gave it an oriental flavor. But its "V" shape cast it as a decidely modern structure, nevertheless.

Nestled in the hollow of the angle formed by the two arms of the "V" was the swimming pool, patio, and gardens. Inside, the angle contained the dining area and bar. The east arm of the "V" was occupied by two small air-conditioned bedrooms—one with a door leading to the patio, a bath, and a kitchen with its own outside door. Beyond was the carport to which was attached a tiny stucco room with bath for the caretaker, Martin Martin. The old man— he could have been one hundred years old for all anyone knew—decorated his cool hovel with modern travel posters. He also had an ancient TV set given to him by the owner of Limeshade Villa, a Kingston business man.

The other side of the "V," the west arm, embraced a living room or sitting area and a large air-conditioned master bedroom and bath. The floors throughout were a waxy white tile enhancing the coolness of the interior. There was no heating system at all except for a hot water mechanism in the kitchen. Nor was there any glass in the windows— only screened louvers or shutters.

Every stick of furniture in the place was modern Danish— imitation leather cushions, mostly black, set into highly polished walnut wood frames for chairs, couches, and stools —similar designs without the black cushions for beds, chests, and whatever else was around. No upholstered, old-fashion fluff here. Generally, the house was cool, comfortable, and uncluttered.

One wall of the dining area was papered with repeat patterns of small blue spirals guaranteed to produce dizziness and nausea when viewed from the bar on the opposite side of the space. All the other walls were plaster, painted a creamy white. There was only one framed picture in the entire house. Unaccountably, it was not a scene of glamorous Jamaica as one might suppose, nor an explosion of Jamaican color, not even a world-famous native attraction such as Dunn's River Falls. No. It was a watercolor reproduction ripped from a travel magazine and depicted a Norwegian fjord as seen from the fantail of a cruise ship.

Give or take a few details this, then, is Limeshade Villa.

There is, however, one peculiarity about the place, or, more accurately, under it, unknown to all except the workmen who actually built the house. And Martin Martin was one of them.

Back around 1957, when the foundation for Limeshade was being dug, Martin and a co-worker discovered an unmarked grave on the building site. Lying face down in the grainy soil, not too far below the surface, was a skeleton. Loosely tangled around its neck were the threaded remnants of a once stout rope. At its feet was a rusty, pitted piece of worn metal that looked like a belt buckle. Plainly inscribed on one edge was a name: "Thos. Sweeney"; on another edge the date: "1720." On still another edge was: "Cyclops." While the fourth edge was inscribed with several indistinguishable letters and what looked like "York."

Nothing was touched in that unearthed grave. Martin and the others quickly covered it over and that was the last anyone ever saw it. The workers spent the rest of the day in a cool palm grove drinking Charlie's rum and gripped in a creeping hysteria, worried as to what God-awful thing would happen to them for having disturbed a dead man's peace after at least two hundred years. Every one of them, except Martin, fled from the job and never returned. And none of them, in the intervening years, ever uttered a word about their experience. A new crew was hired and told nothing. Martin Martin was offered the job of gang boss—foreman—with the promise of retiring to this place as gardener-caretaker. He could hardly turn down such an offer since it guaranteed him a home for life, a better one than he had known throughout his long impoverished existence. Despite his fears and unfaltering belief that "there will come a day, mon, when that dead man will rise and walk in this house," he took the job with the added provision that a TV set be included. It was.

Soon the house, Limeshade Villa, was finished. Martin moved in with his travel posters which he called his "escape from this place plan," and spent many a sleepless night thereafter waiting for the dead man to "rise and walk" and watching TV. Martin Martin, alone, was the only man now alive to know what lay under the house, under Limeshade Villa. In fact, he knew the exact spot—three feet ten and a half inches below the bar.

Jojo clomped into the kitchen sniffing the delicious breakfast air. Still dressed in his oversized crumpled pajamas, he wore a diving mask, loosely strapped to the top of his head, and a pair of swimming fins fixed to his feet.

"I'm Jojo."

Coraleen casually glanced over her shoulder, gave him the once over and continued puttering at the kitchen counter.

"I'm Coraleen Morgan. Now that I know who you are, mon, suppose you tell me what you are."

"I'm a skin diver. And if there are any pieces of eight under any water around here, I'm going to find them."

24

"Well, mon, if any of that loose change shows up in the pool out back, Mr. Martin will vacuum it up for you." Coraleen started to giggle. Annoyed, Jojo shot back, "I'm not talking about swimming pools. I'm talking about the Caribbean Sea—the Spanish Main."

"Oh, mon, that's different. Maybe you better put on a bathing suit before you get your feet wet. Those pajamas aren't going to help much—unless you don't wear nothing at all, mon." Coraleen giggled some more, her eyes sparked and danced like two bright stars.

Jojo was too busy sampling some orange sections and chasing these with a mouthful of freshly diced pineapple to reply. He looked at himself, shrugged, and disappeared into his bedroom. He returned wearing a bathing suit and looking a bit more professional.

Jennifer and Sarilee soon floated into the dining room. By the time Millie appeared a few moments later, Coraleen and the Framer kids were old friends. Mr. Martin had poked his head through the kitchen door, too—not so much to make small talk with Coraleen, but to size up the new people from America.

"Jojo, I think you'd better wake your father. Tell him breakfast is ready. Just say food, that'll get him." Millie knew her Les.

Jojo started out but did not get very far. His father had lurched out of the bedroom into the dining room, half awake—or, more accurately, half asleep—red eyed and rumpled.

"Boy, look at you," Sarilee exclaimed. "Didn't you get any sleep? We did!"

"Obviously not," Jennifer reminded her younger sister. And turning to her father in that imperious manner that could freeze the tropical sun, she added, "You might have at least shaved or combed your hair before coming to the breakfast table."

"Shave? Comb? Who's got time for any of that?"

"Why? What's the rush? Where are we going? Are we leaving already? We just got here!"

"We aren't going anywhere for the next week," Millie snapped. "It's where your father was last night! Traveling!"

"Traveling?"

"Yes, traveling! Walking in his sleep! Having nightmares! Who knows, maybe he was flying too! All night long your father kept shaking me trying to give me a running account of something—of what I haven't the foggiest idea. I told you not to have a rum nightcap Les. Nightcaps are bad enough. But rum and ginger ale? Whew!"

"Nightmares! My foot! Sleepwalking! Baloney! There's a joker around here. O.K., O.K. Which one of you kept me awake the whole night long? And don't tell me I was dreaming! Who was fooling around at the bar?"

"Probably you, Les," Millie cautiously reminded him.

"Me! O.K. Enough is enough. Now who was it? Jojo?

Sarilee? Jennifer? No, not you Jennifer. What about the cook? How about the caretaker? Well? How 'bout an answer? Who's the joker?"

"'Ow about me? Maybe Oi'm the joker, old boy. Me, Thomas Sweeney," chirped the invisible, inaudible character sitting cross-legged on the bar, taking in the scene. "Oi'm a true spirit, Oi ham—wi' special powers, ducks, wi' special powers. Cooooo. This is going to be foine sport.

"'Ang 'im by 'is ruddy neck till dead they said. And 'ang me they did! Me, Thomas Percy Sweeney, captain—oops— late *captain of the good ship* Cyclops—*as sturdy a vessel as ever caught the wind. And for what? Piracy on the 'igh seas they said. Piracy? Cooooo. Oi sought me fortune on the 'igh seas, that's all. Alwize the proper gentleman, was Oi. And Oi never 'armed a living thing, provided of course they treated me wi' proper respect. Oi sailed wi' the best of them, too— Teach, Bonnet, Worley, Mary Read, Anne Bonny. Ah, Anne Bonny! There was a winsome lass! Cooooo. She'd pop your eyeballs clear out of your 'ead, wi' 'er fingers, too, if she didn't like your looks. Hoi! Anne, love, wherever ye are, the best to ye.*

"'Ow many years 'as hit been? Two hundred? Two hundred and fifty? Two hundred and fifty-two, to be exact. Aye. February 20, 1720, right to the very day. And a foine bright day hit was. Cooooo.

"Oi fooled the King's bloody own that day. They murdered me body and left hit quivering and swinging in the noon breeze. But they couldn't murder me spirit. Hit was too large. Oi should've climbed out of me lonely grave when those rascals found me tired old bones.

"Oi've been patient all these years, putting up wi' every inconvenience trying to get me heternal rest. Hits not easy wi' this small tavern 'ard over'ead—wi' all that blessed rum so close and me unable to touch a drop. No matter. Now, Oi, Thomas Percy Sweeney 'as 'ad hit wi' the likes of these Yankee travelers here. Oi'm going to 'ave me fun. Cooooo. Oi'm 'oisting me hanchor! Hoi! Yaaaaaaaaaa!"

Sweeney stood up on the bar waving his great cutlass back and forth. He made ferocious, menacing, blood-curdling cries. He was a magnificent, threatening figure. Unfortunately, no one could see him or hear him. Sweeney was as he said he was—a spirit—an ethereal creature from a world beyond—a ghost who somehow or other lingered on much past its time, refusing to lie down and be quiet, so to speak.

Nevertheless, there he was, however invisible, appearing exactly as he did in life, a huge hulk of a seadog; an eighteenth-century fashion plate from the tip of the ostrich plume that dangled from his brown tricorn to the silver buckles on his shiny black leather red-heeled boots. The rest of him was silk, satin, and velvet. Two flintlock pistols and a dagger were tucked into a sash wrapped around his considerable midsection. A bearded, swashbuckling, large-nosed, thick-lipped, scarred, and partially toothed giant, Thomas Sweeney looked like what a pirate is supposed to look like—terrifying—a splendid ghost in every respect.

29

"One more time. Who's the joker in the crowd?" Les demanded. They all stared at him as if he had lost his mind, including Coraleen who had just arrived at the dining room table with a plate loaded with buttered toast. Les glared at her. "Who are you?"

"Father," offered Jennifer with studied impatience, "meet Coraleen Morgan. You'd better be nice to her or else you may not eat as well as the rest of us. Coraleen," she continued dryly, "meet our cruise director." Coraleen tilted her head to one side, squeezed her eyes shut, and smiled sweetly.

Millie burst out laughing. "For God's sake, Les, go get a bathrobe or something and have some breakfast. You're too ridiculous."

Sweeney leaped off the bar making sure not to rattle anything inside. He could do just that—rattle things. Anyway, he tiptoed over to Les and put his arm around his shoulder. Les inexplicably shuddered for a brief second. *"Let's 'ave hit, Governor. Tell them hall about hit. Cooooo. Oi can't wait to 'ear it meself."*

"Ridiculous am I. Well, let me tell you what happened. Maybe it'll refresh someone's memory."

30

"*Cooooo. That's a good one, that is.*"

"First of all I got up to turn off the pool lights. The whole house seemed to be lit up. And I like to sleep in the dark, not in a spooky green glow."

"*Spooky! Cooooo. Oi'll remember that one, too, Oi will.*"

"Well, I turned them off all right. The switch is in the kitchen in case anyone's interested." No one was. They were all too busy eating. "Right then and there someone sneaked into the dining room. Whichever one of you it was must have bumped the bar because I heard every bottle and glass inside rattle."

"*Oi'm sorry about that, Governor. Truly Oi ham. Oi'm usually very light on me feet, Oi ham.*"

"Les, honey, how many nightcaps did you have?" Millie asked without looking up from her bacon and eggs.

"Let me finish, will you?"

"*Aye, woman, let yer lord and master, finish,*" Sweeney added, in true male chauvinist style. It's a good thing Millie could not hear that last remark. It would have sent her into a creeping rage.

Les went on. "I rushed into the dining room figuring to surprise whoever it was. But no one was there. Somehow or other they got away. I stayed a few minutes in the dark. There wasn't a sound. I went back to bed. No sooner did I hit the sack the whole thing started all over again. The pool lights went on. I got up again to shut them off. I heard the

31

bottles and glasses rattling around in the bar. I checked it out. No one. I went back to bed. This happened a few more times. I even checked out the bedrooms. Everyone seemed to be asleep—or faking it. It was hard to tell in the dark. I tried to shake you awake, Millie, a few times, to let you in on what was going on. No dice. You kept swatting me away like I was a dive-bombing mosquito. Maybe it was you all along.

"Finally, I thought I was going nuts, or having a wide awake nightmare, when all of a sudden I heard the bottles and glasses again. Not only that, someone was pushing or pulling the bar! I could hear it rocking back and forth and scraping the floor. This time I had him—or her—one of you—or maybe all of you.

"So I crept out there nice and quietlike. Then I grabbed for the bar. I missed. No one. Just then those blasted pool lights went on again. I ran into the kitchen. No one. This time I didn't turn the lights off. Like a crazy man I ran back into the dining room. And what do you think I saw. I was right. No one was there but the bar had been moved. It was about six inches back from where it had been. I could tell by the marks on the floor. Then the lights went off again. That's when I quit."

"*Oi'm sorry about that, too, Governor. Hall that while Oi was trying to pick meself hup out of me grave. Hit took a bit a doing you know. Oi 'adn't been hup and around since the day oi was 'anged. Oi turned on the lights has well. Right from me grave Oi did, too. Cooooo. Oi don't know me own strength. 'Ow else could Oi see.*" Sweeney roared. *His whole ghostly frame shook with laughter. Plainly, he had enjoyed the night—at Lester Framer's expense.*

32

"See for yourselves," Les said. "Take a look at the bar. It's been moved."

"Where to?" asked Jojo. "It's still in the same place."

"It can't be!"

"It is!"

"Hits in the same place, me bucko, the same place. Oi moved hit back. Heverything in hits proper place Oi always say."

"Listen!" Les was furious. "A joke is a joke. You've had your fun. I'm going back to bed. I'm bushed. Wake me at noon. Maybe then I'll decide whether or not to have lunch with you all."

Les stretched, kicked off the light cover, and vaulted out of bed. It was noon. No one had to wake him. He felt good, refreshed. He was ready to forget last night's confusion and this morning's irritation.

"It just goes to show you," he mumbled with a mouthful of toothpaste, "I really need a vacation. Man! Was I wound up—tighter than a spool of plastic tape. I really let those characters of mine get to me. Maybe I did dream the whole thing. Could be!"

Les put on a bathing suit and pranced out of the house in time to join everyone on the pool apron for lunch.

The Framers had not planned anything special for Sunday. All they intended to do on this their first full day in Jamaica was to rid their bones of the fierce winter they had just left behind—sunbathe, swim in their pool, sunbathe, swim again, eat, nap, drink tropical fruit punches and otherwise loll around.

Jojo, fully equipped in his skin-diving outfit, had spent the entire morning retrieving quarters that Sarilee kept tossing into the pool. He was practicing for bigger game—diving for pieces of eight—in the sea. Jennifer, covered from head to foot with a creamy suntan lotion remained immobile, stretched out on a chaise longue. Every so often she turned over. Other than that and rising for a bite of lunch, she did not move a muscle. Even Sarilee, having tired of training Jojo, finally smeared herself with suntan lotion and began the same sunbathing routine that Jennifer stiffly pursued.

Millie and Les swam a few laps once in a while. But for the better part of the afternoon they slept in the shade of separate lime trees.

Sweeney, sitting with his back against the house, placidly surveyed the listless Framers, now motionless in the heat of the sun and scattered around the pool like fallen bowling pins.

"Oi don't know why they should 'ave hit so good, Oi don't. And me. What about me? This is me hanniversary, hit is. Oi think we should all celebrite me 'anging."

34

Sweeney jumped into the pool and floated around for a while. Bored, he climbed and paced back and forth on the diving board. "This 'ere plank reminds me of the good old days," he mused. "Only hit's got too much spring."

Suddenly he quit pacing. "Oi've got hit," he declared. "We'll drink to hit. Hoi. Everyone up," he commanded. "Let's 'ave a mug in 'onor of me 'anging day."

Les stirred. "Millie? Psst. Millie? You awake?"

"Barely."

"You thirsty?"

"Come to think of it, yes."

"I'm parched. Maybe you can get Coraleen to fix a pitcher of some nice cold punch."

"Good idea," Sarilee piped up. "I'll go."

A few minutes later, Sarilee called out, "We need a couple of limes."

"Cooooo. Oi can see to that," Sweeney responded. He raced over to the two lime trees that stood side by side, shading Les and Millie.

As Les lazily reached over his head to pick off a few ripe limes, the old pirate grabbed both trees and shook them violently. A bushel of limes cascaded down on Les and Millie. Most of them bounced off their heads.

35

"Hey, Les," Millie screamed, "what are you trying to do? Just a couple of limes. That's all. We don't need the whole tree."

"I didn't do anything. I didn't even touch a leaf."

"Listen, Les, if this is your idea of revenge because of last night, it isn't funny—not funny at all."

No one had seen the trees shake. Coraleen and Sarilee had been in the kitchen. Jennifer was sunbathing—eyes shut. Jojo was spread-eagled on a patch of grass. A wet towel covered his face. Now they all crowded around looking at the mass of fallen limes. *Sweeney, very pleased with himself, leaned against one of the trees and smiled. For good measure he quickly shook a small branch and several more limes hit the ground.* Coraleen picked up three of them and returned to the kitchen.

"There, did you see that?" Les bawled. "I didn't even touch them."

"What did you expect," Millie retorted. "You upset the tree in the first place."

"Have it your way. But I'll tell you one thing, you can't blame it on my nightcaps and you can't blame it on the breeze. There isn't any breeze. If you ask me, this place is haunted."

"Oi never thought of that, Governor. 'Aunted did you say? Coooo. Oi'll 'ave to keep on me guard, what with spooks running amuck."

Martin Martin, the ancient caretaker, came upon the scene in time to hear one word, "haunted." Having first dismissed the events of this morning—last night, to be exact—as an "American family prank," he now quickly retreated to his hovel behind the carport, slammed the door and locked it.

Coraleen returned with a pitcher of inviting punch. Sarilee offered a toast, "To Limeshade Villa, the haunted house."

"Here, here," they all chorused, including Les who decided not to get up-tight again. "To Limeshade Villa, the haunted house."

"To me 'anging, me darlings, to me 'anging."

At that, Sweeney broke into a raucous fit of laughter that nearly broke the sound barrier—the barrier between his world and the Framers' world. For at that moment a strong, cool wind disturbed the languid air and swirled up into the trees.

Another lime fell. The startled Framers gaped at the sky all around them. It was cloudless, brilliant, and blue.

All was still again.

"There wasn't even a breeze before," Les whispered.

MONDAY
February 21, 1972

There was no sign of the Framers. Half the morning was gone and they were still asleep. Actually, there was no pressing reason for them to have risen earlier. A warm, persistent, demoralizing rain was soaking the entire northeast coast of Jamaica. The only thing on the Framers' morning schedule was a trip into town to do some marketing.

Coraleen was in a hurry, however. There was not enough food in the house to feed a stray cat, let alone a ravenous family of five, Martin Martin, and herself. She had arrived on schedule—7:00 A.M.—and somehow or other spent two and a half hours, mopping, dusting, and purposefully dropping things in a vain effort to wake someone up. In between,

Coraleen kept trying to light the gas-heated stove. But the pilot light—the small jet flame in the center used to light the four burners—did not work right. It kept going out every time she turned on the gas to one of the burners. It was as if someone kept blowing it out. She tried to hold her breath each time thinking she was breathing too hard on the small flame. That did not work either. In fact, nothing would have worked. *Sweeney saw to that. He continued to blow it out.* Coraleen continued to relight it until she finally won.

And the Framers slept on.

During the night and not too many hours before Coraleen arrived to battle the stove, Sweeney had made a halfhearted attempt to disturb the sleeping family. He was not very original. He played with the pool lights again, flicking them on and off—somewhat absent-mindedly—while trying to think of more terrifying things to do. Unfortunately, he was frustrated by a hammering, slashing thunder and lightning storm. If anyone had seen the on-again, off-again glow of the underwater pool lights, they would have surely assumed it to be streaks of lightning momentarily brightening the dark wet night. Besides, Sweeney knew that no amount of ghostly rattling could be heard above the crashing noises of the storm.

42

For a while, he sulked, sitting cross-legged on the bar, his large hairy head resting heavily in his hands. Sweeney felt powerless. Occasionally, he would climb down from his perch with a great sigh, stretch and wander aimlessly about making mean and hollow sounds that no one in the living world could hear—storm or no storm. Each time he would return to the bar, rattle it a bit—more out of a sense of ghostly duty than anything else—climb up, sit down, and continue to sulk.

As daybreak approached, the wild storm had quit. Only the steady rain remained.

"Hit would 'ave been a foine night for 'aunting," he moaned, "if that racket 'ad only stopped. Right now Oi'd settle for a bit of grog and one of me own kind."

"Psssst. Sweeney."

The startled pirate stiffened.

"Sweeney?"

"'Ere now," he answered, as he cautiously slid down behind the bar, putting aside his huge cutlass and drawing both his pistols.

"Ooz there?"

"Me."

"And ooz me?"

"Me! You old rascal!"

Not one, but two ghostly women passed through the louver doors near the bar. One was a slender, raven-haired beauty attired in a long skirted suit and riding boots. If it were not for the whip she carried, she would have seemed shy, almost childlike. There was no doubt that she was once a lady of quality.

The other was a plump, disheveled character dressed in a short jacket and wide, loose-fitting sailor's pants. A long, thick leather belt swept downward across her ample bosom. A short sword dangled from a loop at the lower end. In her right hand was a battle-ax.

"Well, Oi'll be!" Sweeney cried out. "Anne Bonny! You're a sight for me old oiyes. Where'd ye come from? And ooz the lass wi' ye?"

"Oi couldn't sleep hearing you was hup and about craving companionship. So, ducks, Oi came hall the way from London Town to bring you a spot of cheer. And this 'ere 'igh born lidy is me good chum, Annie Palmer. She seen ye shake those old trees. Not knowing anything about ye, Annie came to me to mike proper inquiries. Oi gave 'er an earful, Oi did. 'Aven't ye ever 'eard of Annie?"

"Can't say as Oi've 'ad."

"Oi suppose not, ye being indisposed since the day ye was 'anged and she being murdered in 'er bed, poor thing, long after ye was put in your grave. Annie, meet Captain Thomas Sweeney, has foine a black-hearted cutthroat as Oi've ever 'ad the pleasure to sile with. Sweeney, meet Annie Palmer, the White Witch of Rose Hall."

44

"White Witch? Ooz a witch? This 'ere lass? Coooo. Come off it, love."

"Aye, she's a sweet one, she is. There's blood on 'er everlasting soul. Tell 'im hall about, sweetie. Tell 'im."

Sweeney listened with horror as Annie Palmer unfolded a history of such cruelty and vile passions that at times he found it hard to believe. Anne Bonny assured him that every word was the truth.

"And Oi thought Oi did 'orrible things to me fellow men," *Sweeney croaked.*

Mistress of Rose Hall, Jamaica's greatest late eighteenth-century north coast sugar plantation, Annie Palmer stabbed, poisoned, and strangled three husbands—and countless lovers—to become the undisputed ruler of the estate and more than a thousand slaves that labored there. She used her whip at the slightest provocation. And as she watched with intense excitement and pleasure, many a slave died at her whipping posts—men and women alike. Often their heads were severed from their battered bodies and staked to a bamboo pole to rot in the Jamaica sun. Annie finally met her untimely death in a mighty black slave rebellion that shook the island and gutted magnificent Rose Hall. All that was in 1833. Now, in 1972, Rose Hall is a rebuilt tourist attraction inhabited by no one except some care-

46

takers, various workers, and Annie Palmer, whose restless spirit still stalks the place.

"There, what did Oi tell ye, Sweeney," Anne Bonny happily declared after her friend had finished supplying all of the miserable details of her wicked life, "ain't she a good one?"

Sweeney stared at both of them. He seemed incapable of making a sound.

Finally, he spoke. "And what would ye 'ave wi' me, Annie Palmer?"

"It seemed to me," she said, "that you might visit me at the Great House. We could have such fine walks together. You are so big and strong, the kind of giant I could love forever."

"Love forever? You? Me? Get out of me sight," Sweeney howled. "Oi wouldn't take hup wi' the loikes of ye if me loife depended on hit—which is no longer the case. Oi did some 'orrible things, Oi did. But that was in the course of me business. Oi never murdered or tortured another for pleasure. And Oi was alwize proper wi' any lidy, 'igh or low, Oi took at sea or elsewhere. You're mad, Annie Palmer. Away wi' ye. Oi never want to set me oiyes on ye again—not through all eternity. Away."

Annie Palmer backed up. She never expected to meet another spirit larger or stronger than herself. But Sweeney was overpowering in his disgust. Annie Palmer returned, alone, to the Great House of Rose Hall.

"Now look what ye've done, Sweeney. Ye could 'ave lived

like a king in that 'ouse instead of like a common spirit in this rat 'ole."

"Does it matter?" Sweeney asked. "You and me, we are spooks. Oi've no kick wi' you, Anne Bonny. We are still shipmites. We 'ave a special understanding. But that other one, that friend of yours, she's not for us."

"'Ere comes the daylight, Sweeney. Oi'd best be going. But don't ye worry none, ducks, Oi'll come anytoime ye call."

"Oi've been dead two hundred fifty-two years and one day has of roight now. And hall this toime Oi've been by meself. Oi thank ye for your visit, Anne Bonny. By the by, 'ow many years 'as hit been for you?"

"A lidy never tells 'er age, ducks. Never!"

Marketing and lunch had long since past—dinner too. Coraleen had gone home a couple of hours ago. Martin Martin was still locked in his room. His worry over the house being "haunted" had subsided somewhat, but not without the help of a bottle of Charlie's rum. Now he was preparing to turn on his television set to watch an evening movie.

The rain was still there. All day long, low, dark watery clouds swept over Limeshade Villa. There, directly overhead, they broke, soaking the scruffy terrain beyond the villa walls, turning the loose gravel into a mess of shallow, muddy ponds. Every so often the drenching rain would slacken. The sun would suddenly appear and disappear. Heavy humid steam would rise from the ground and puddles giving an unearthly, if not hellish, cast to the scene. And just when everyone thought it was all over, blinding sheets of rain would slam into the roof and tear at the foliage around the patio.

"Some vacation," Les complained as he fooled around with a small portable transistor radio. Jojo was off in a corner deeply absorbed in a book he had borrowed from the Aspetuck Public Library: "Lives of the Notorious Pirates, True Tales of the Spanish Main." He did not hear his father. Neither did Jennifer and Sarilee. They were concentrating too hard on a game of Scrabble—all tied up at 73 points each. Millie was writing on a pad of yellow blue-lined paper fastened to a clipboard.

"Hey! Listen to this! 'The Hit Parade'—Jamaica style. This baritone is reading today's obituary. It's kind of like a newscast—who died and where to send the flowers—all in alphabetical order!"

"Can't you get something else," Millie pleaded. "It gives me the creeps."

"O.K. O.K. But did you catch the background music? Very restful." Les turned the dial.

"Hey. Here's another station. The man said Miami. Not bad for a dime store radio. We are picking up the U.S.A. It's a boxing match. No it isn't. The guy just got knocked out. Stay tuned the man says for big time wrestling to be followed by a complete rebroadcast of a Miami Dolphin-Washington Redskin game. Say! You know what? This is a twenty-four-hour sportcast station. Beautiful!"

"Yuk," was Millie's reaction. "I'm going to bed."

"At nine o'clock?"

"I've got things to do. See!" Millie confronted Les with her clipboard. Neatly lettered in large block figures at the top of the yellow blue-lined pad was "G.A.A.L.L.S." As she huffily left the room, Millie added, "I've got my own sports program to figure out."

Martin Martin was seated on his small bed fiddling with the TV tuning dial *when Sweeney floated through the locked door and joined him—on the bed.*

The old ghost had been wandering in and around the busy Framers, peering first over Jojo's shoulder to see what he was reading; and then puzzling over the Scrabble game and Millie's clipboard. All the while he gradually assumed an air of creeping disgust and studied nonchalance, fearful that someone might learn of his terrible weakness. He could not read.

Sweeney did not like Les's radio either. Not the sound of it.

50

Not the disembodied voice that came from it. Sweeney cupped his hands over his ears and stalked outside.

Now he sat with Mr. Martin as the old man gazed blankly at his TV set. An old movie—a saga of the sea—was beginning to unfold its romantic tale.

Two powerful wooden sailing ships were closing in on each other. Both vessels clearly showed their colors: a Spanish flag on one; a British flag on the other. The Spanish ship opened fire with a great starboard salvo. The Britisher, untouched, kept coming on. Suddenly, she struck her colors and hoisted a new flag—a black flag with a white death's head—a skull and bones. And just as suddenly she answered the Spaniard with a devastating broadside of her own. The Spaniard seemed to come apart.

"'Ere now," Sweeney exclaimed, "this his more like hit. Things 'aven't changed much, 'ave they? Oi wonder oo they are. Oi didn't see a familiar face."

Martin Martin took a long draft from his bottle of Charlie's rum.

The Spanish ship continued to shoot back. Now the pirate came apart. Fires raged unchecked on both vessels. *Sweeney watched with burning excitement.* Men screamed and died. Splintered masts, torn canvas, and a tangle of ropes and pulleys littered the decks. Both ships came alongside each other. Grappling hooks soared over the rails and gunnels of both ships locking them securely together. Astonishingly, all of the dead and wounded seemed to come to life. And joining the living, they all grabbed ropes and tried to swing aboard the other's ship. Brandishing swords, pistols, sticks, and bare fists, they all met in the middle, every one of them.

"This is impossible—ridiculous!" Sweeney shouted, leaping to his feet and waving his own cutlass around. Martin Martin took another swig from his bottle. *"Dead men live again? No one blistered by the flame? And look at the scum. Look at them, Oi say!" Sweeney was appealing to Mr. Martin.* Unaware, the old man watched the roaring adventure on the television screen. *"Bah! Baboons! That's what they are! Baboons swinging on their ruddy vines. Oi never allowed a crew of mine to swing around like that—anywise, not hall of them at once!"*

Sweeney pounded the top of the TV. Martin Martin, still unaware, blamed the rumbling on the ships' guns. *Sweeney punched the screen itself.* The ghostly force knocked out the picture replacing it with a vibrating pattern of zigzagging bands.

"Static," Martin mumbled. *Sweeney was mystified by the loss of the picture.* Martin slapped the TV. The picture returned. But only for a second. *Sweeney punched the screen again.* The zigzagging bands reappeared. *Still perplexed, Sweeney rattled the set, rocking it back and forth.* The old caretaker gulped and sucked the stale air as he watched the set seemingly rock by itself. The fright of the moment was not lost on Martin Martin. He sat stiffly on the bed, his back pressed flat against the wall. The half empty bottle of Charlie's rum slipped from his shaking hand and hit the cement floor, its contents slowly trickling out as *Sweeney continued to rock the TV set.* The bands that flickered across the screen zigzagged more furiously than before.

52

Sweeney turned a dial. The TV went off altogether. Martin saw the dial spin. Yet, he did not want to believe what he saw. He just sat there, frozen, as the terror of the moment began to settle on him. Finally, with some courage, he gingerly reached for the dial. He turned it. The movie appeared once more. The ships were still locked in their fiery struggle. The hostile crews still dangled on their ropes.

"Rot!" Sweeney bellowed, pounding the set again before turning it off. Again, Martin reached out, hesitated, and then quickly turned the TV on.

"Oi said hoff and hoff it'll be." Sweeney turned the TV off, rattling the set for good measure.

Martin Martin bolted for the door. It was locked. He forgot about that. In his panic to get out, he nearly tore out the knob. The old man fell backward onto his bed, panting.

"It's the dead one," he moaned. "He's up and about—in here!"

Martin picked up his partially full bottle of rum by its neck and whipped the air around him.

"Get away from me you devil—get away!" After thoroughly drenching himself with the rest of the rum, Martin flung the bottle at the door. *Sweeney picked it up and tossed it back on the bed.* Martin was frantic. *Sweeney deftly unlocked the door.* The old man made another attempt to escape the tiny room. He launched himself *as Sweeney obligingly opened the door.* Martin Martin hurtled to freedom screaming into the raining night, "Dead men walk! Dead men walk!"

Sweeney shrugged. "Cooooo. 'E'll never come back to this place again. Oi banished 'im proper, Oi did. Oi think Oi'll work me charms on me Yankee visitors."

But Sweeney did not pursue his quarry immediately. Instead, the ghostly buccaneer switched on the TV and watched as both vessels slipped beneath the flat sea leaving behind a few survivors who clung to floating debris—presumably to go on living and fighting at some later date.

"What's all that racket outside?" Millie called out.

"What racket? You're hearing things, Millie. We didn't hear anything. Did we hear anything, kids? Maybe it was the rain."

Silence. No one answered. Jennifer, Sarilee, and Jojo heard nothing—not even their father who was casually thumbing through a dog-eared whodunit paperback left behind by a previous vacationer.

The girls were numb with concentration. Their Scrabble battle was still all tied up—only now the score was 103 to 103. Jennifer was about to sting her sister with a 36-point triple-word score, however.

Les put the book down. He decided not to read it. Some

vandal had neatly torn out the last four or five pages. Les would never know who did it, whatever the crime. He stretched and wistfully glanced over at the bar, then at his son.

"How's that book you've got there Jojo? Interesting? Jojo! Are you there? Is anybody there? Here? Anywhere?"

"Oi ham, Governor," replied Sweeney. The ancient pirate was sitting on the bar in his usual cross-legged position. He had walked out on the movie when both ships went to the bottom. "Let them swim for hit," he grumbled, "the ruddy baboons."

"I hear you, Dad. I hear you. This stuff is so great I can't put it down. Did you know that guys like Avery, Martel, Low, Rackam, and Teach—that was Blackbeard—they were all pirate captains—roamed up and down the East Coast—you know, Boston, New York, Philly, Long Island Sound, the Carolinas."

"Nope."

"Here's a beaut. Take this Captain Sweeney, for example—Thomas Percy Sweeney."

"Sweeney? Did Oi 'ear the lad say Sweeney?"

"He was a regular juvenile delinquent. According to this Sweeney was a young hoodlum on the Thames River wharves. By the time he was eleven he had been busted a couple of times and thrown into the workhouse for "larceny, malicious assault upon innocent persons, trafficking in stolen properties and other assorted mischiefs.""

"That's a lie." Sweeney was indignant. *"Oi was born in Jamaica and left a poor babe orphan in London Town—merry old England—wi' no 'ome, no proper heducation, no one to look after me. Oi was left to me own devices."*

"When he was thirteen," Jojo went on, "he was taken out of the workhouse and put aboard a Boston-bound merchant ship—hand-picked because of his unusual size. That was in 1698."

"That's a lie, too. Oi was a big one all right, but Oi was clever. Oi 'and-picked meself. Oi escaped and 'id aboard a large vessel. She went to sea wi' me in 'er stinking bilge. Cooooo. Oi remember 'er well. She was the Star of Bombay. No merchantman was she. Oi picked a rotten slaver 'eading for Madagascar."

"Sounds exciting Jojo." Les yawned. "We'll continue tomorrow."

"No wait, Dad. You've got to hear the rest of this."

"Aye, Governor. Let the lad go on."

"O.K. Jojo. There's not much else to do, Let's have the rest of it."

"Well, one thing led to another. By the time Sweeney was twenty, he had his own ship and a price on his head. All in all he spent the next fifteen years terrorizing the West Indies, the East Coast, the Indian Ocean, and the West African Coast. Sweeney plundered, tortured, murdered, and generally tore up the sea lanes and what little coastal towns got in his way."

"More lies," Sweeney protested. "That was me livelihood. Hit was a suitable trade considering that Oi 'ad to make me own way. And Oi was an expert hat hit, Oi was."

"It says here, too, that Sweeney was known as a perfect gentleman when it came to the ladies; that he became very rich; that he salted away a fortune somewhere between the Rio Grande River and Frenchman's Cove and that it remains undiscovered to this very day. Well, at least until 1935 when this book was published."

"Cooooo. The ladies. Oi never 'armed a one in me hentire loife. But oo said Oi was rich! Rot! Oi was not alwize a pauper. That's true. But if Oi 'ad any treasure 'id away, Oi would 'ave built me a castle, filled hit wi' wives and stayed there until Oi died of old age instead of the way Oi did. Oi never would 'ave sailed again—never!"

"Anyway, the most interesting part of all this, Dad, is Sweeney's finish."

"Cooooo. Tell me laddie."

"Sweeney was in New York getting a ship fitted out—that was in January, 1720—when the Crown issued a proclamation granting amnesty to all pirates provided their captains were included when they turned themselves in. Sweeney figured it was a trick to capture the leaders. He convinced his crew that they would be executed as soon as they turned themselves in; and that the best thing to do was to sail out of New York, ready or not, wintry seas or not. They did. But they hadn't gone very far when most of the crew mutinied, threw overboard those who refused, and put Sweeney in chains."

58

"Aye. What treachery!"

"Then they returned to New York to accept the offer of amnesty. The day they tied up the entire crew was given a full pardon for piracy. It was like a New Year's present. Then they were promptly arrested for mutiny. A week later, every one of them—about thirty—everyone but Sweeney, that is —was hanged, convicted of mutiny."

"Aye that's the truth of hit."

"Sweeney was never pardoned. Instead, he was packed off in chains to Jamaica where they threw the book at him. Here's the sentence:

> The Court, having duly considered of the evidence which hath been given for and against you the said Thomas Percy Sweeney, and having debated the several circumstances of the case, it is adjudged that you, the said Thomas Percy Sweeney, are guilty of the piracy wherewith you stand accused. And the Court doth accordingly pass sentence that you, the said Thomas Percy Sweeney, be carried to prison from whence you came, and from thence to the place of execution, where you are to be hanged by the neck till you shall be dead, dead, dead; and God have Mercy on your soul. Given under our hands this 19th day of February, Anno Dom. 1720, signed

CHARLES DOWLING	ROBERT COLE
WILLIAM KEYS	HENRY BREWSTER
WILLIAM WALKER	GEORGE EVANS
JOHN BROOKE	EDWARD WHITFORD

"Sweeney was hanged at noon the next day, 252 years ago yesterday."

60

"Oi never thought Oi'd 'ear me sentence again."

"And here's the strangest part. Sweeney was hanged on a hot, still day. There was absolutely no breeze. Yet, for three days after he died on the gallows, Sweeney's body refused to quit swaying and spinning in a mysterious breeze that wasn't there. The royal governor who had ordered the body to dangle in public for seven days now ordered Sweeney cut down immediately and buried in an unmarked grave somewhere along the unpopulated north coast."

"Right 'ere, me buckos, right 'ere."

"The executioner reported that minutes before Sweeney's life was choked from him, the pirate whispered to him that he was only dying temporarily; that he will walk again and worry this island until the end of time."

"Aye. That's true."

"Take a look at this illustration. It shows a mob of people, some on their knees praying, watching Sweeney being cut down. His hands are tied in front of him and the piece of rope is pretty tight around his neck."

" 'Ere, let's 'ave a look at that!"

Sweeney jumped off the bar. He yanked the book out of Jojo's hands. For a second or two, the open book remained suspended in mid air—long enough to shock Les, Jojo, and the girls. Suddenly, the book soared through the air, slammed against the bar and jarred a couple of glasses hard enough to break them. *Sweeney did not like that particular picture of himself.*

61

Millie rushed out of the bedroom. "Now tell me you didn't hear that racket! What's going on out here anyway? Just because this house doesn't belong to us is no reason to feel free to break it up!"

No one answered. Les and his children stared open-mouthed at the bar, the crumpled book, the broken glass, and nothing more. Finally, Les cranked up his courage and whispered, "What was the name of that character you were telling me about?"

"Sweeney. Captain Thomas Sweeney. Why?"

"I've got a weird feeling that we've got a visitor."

"Sweeney?"

"Sweeney."

"Who in blazes is Sweeney," Millie demanded. "I don't see any visitors around here!"

"A ghost!" they chorused.

"You're all putting me on. There is no such thing!"

"'*Ere now, me dear, Oi resent that.*" *And to prove his presence, Sweeney picked up the book.* Millie watched—so did everyone else—as the floating book glided across the room and came to rest at her bare feet.

"*What say you now?*" *Sweeney asked.*

62

"It's a trick," Millie insisted.

"*A trick!*" Sweeney picked up the book and flung it back at the bar. Another glass fell over and broke.

"A ghost," Millie agreed.

TUESDAY
February 22, 1972

Coraleen did not believe in ghosts—"duppies" she called them. Coraleen was a modern Jamaican, an independent Jamaican; free of foreign overlords these past ten years; free of ignorance; free of the intimidating superstitions that enslaved so much of her island for three hundred years. She worked hard and efficiently. She saved her money and kept the men in her life in line. Young Coraleen Morgan was no easy mark—not for tourists, not for duppies.

Sweeney had sensed this large spirit that lived within her— a spirit greater than his own—and had quickly decided not to tangle with the likes of Coraleen Morgan. In fact, he had a good idea that Coraleen Morgan was no pushover. He caught the drift of that when she refused to give up re-lighting the stove's pilot light each time he blew it out. In the end and although it was a minor thing, it was he, Sweeney, the duppy with all the time in the world—eternity, no less—who gave in. Besides, his whole aim was short range; to get rid of the Framers and send them back to where they came from, the sooner the better. They were the interlopers, not Coraleen. They and their kind were the disruptive force in his unearthly existence. So was Martin Martin for that matter. Tourists were too noisy. Martin Martin knew too much. He had already rid himself of the old caretaker.

In any event, when Coraleen arrived this sunny morning, she was rushed by a near incoherent mob of weary Framers babbling something about an invisible "thing or ghost"—"dead nut" as Sarilee colorfully described it—who threw books, broke glasses, turned pool lights on and off, and probably shook lime trees among other things.

"In this house?" she queried. "Duppies live in old stone castles with great bats flying around; not in a place like this." Coraleen was willing to acknowledge the possible existence of a ghost. But while she still did not believe in ghosts, the young Jamaican did not want to antagonize her temporary employers. If the Framers insisted there was a ghost, then there was a ghost—maybe.

"Yes. Here in this house. Last night." The Framers were all yelling at once.

"Aye. 'Ere in this 'ouse. Last night." Sweeney would not be denied. "And the night before," he added.

"Why would a duppy pick on this house?" Coraleen did not want to give in altogether. Perhaps they were working up some kind of practical joke. It would not be the first time.

"Why not?" Sweeney wanted to know.

"Who knows?" the Framers offered, addressing themselves to Coraleen, still unable to hear the invisible pirate.

"Well, mon, the only duppy between here and Mo Bay is Annie Palmer. It's in all the books. But I don't know anyone that has ever seen that white witch." Coraleen wagged her turbanned head from side to side. Vacationing American families came in assorted lots. The Framers, in Coraleen's estimation, were a little difficult to understand—more so than most of those who rented Limeshade Villa. Yet, she could put up with it. That was part of her job. She was determined to go about her business and at the same time hoped that the week went by quickly. Finally, glancing at the ceiling in exasperation, Coraleen walked into the kitchen and out the door to look for Martin Martin. She had a few chores for him. *Sweeney followed her.*

"Martin. Mr. Martin. Come, mon, it is time to greet the sun. Come meet the duppy, too."

"Do you want to know what I think?" Les asked Millie.

"Nope," Millie dreamily responded. "And do I have to know right this minute?"

The two of them were stretched out on the soft warm sand of a small out-of-the-way beach. They had scouted around for just such a beach after breakfast and found it a couple of miles off the main road not far from Oracabessa. It was one of those idyllic, half-moon stretches of sand ringed by tall, graceful coconut palms used for television commercials by the Jamaica Tourist Board. And the Framers had this one all to themselves—or so they thought.

Sweeney had gone along for the ride after making sure that Martin Martin had not returned. Perched on the roof of the car he became a ghostly sight-seer. Now he lurked in the shade of the palms—not that being either in the shade or the sun made any difference to him.

Overhead, the hot midday sun tested the layers of suntan lotion Les and Millie had smeared all over themselves. Once in a while a cooling, delicate breeze would rustle the great palm leaves.

Jennifer found her own lonely spot of sand and hoped for a perfect tan. Between Jennifer and her parents was a wall of

68

towels, cameras, a couple of flight bags filled with odds and ends, a pile of clothing, and a picnic basket. Sarilee and Jojo snorkeled in the mild blue-green surf looking for exotic shells and pieces of eight. All they seemed to accumulate were shells.

"Well, since you don't want to know what I think, I'll tell you. I think we've got a poltergeist back at Limeshade Villa."

"A what!"

"A poltergeist."

"What's that?"

"A ghost that throws things, knocks on walls, tables, doors, and likes to rattle objects not nailed down."

"If I hadn't seen what I saw last night, Les, I would say that you had flipped. Could be we are all crazy."

"No. I don't think so, Millie, although it sure seems so on such a beautiful, peaceful day."

"Maybe it'll go away.

"Maybe. But I've got a hunch that it won't go away until we do. And I still have that weird feeling we're dealing with that pirate Jojo was reading about—Sweeney."

"This is ridiculous," Millie proclaimed. "Listen to us! Two normal, intelligent people matter-of-factly discussing our ghost like ghosts were everyday happenings; like everyone knows that ghosts or poltergeists are for real—that there are two worlds, ours and *theirs*. We must be crazy. Last night never happened. It was a bad dream. You can talk yourself into poltergeists if you like. I'm going swimming. If I were you I'd do the same thing. It'll cool you off."

Millie pulled herself upright and fled into the water. "Your father is working himself and the rest of us into a nightmare —his nightmare. I know, I know, I agreed last night that there was a ghost in the room. But that was last night. There just has to be a rational explanation. This is the twentieth century!" Millie was appealing to Sarilee and Jojo.

"Anyhow, do you know what your father has decided?"

"No. What?" asked Jennifer who had joined the group in the water.

"He has decided there's a poltergeist named Sweeney back at the ranch."

"Cool," said Jennifer.

"Wow!" gasped the two snorkelers. "What's that?"

"A ghost with an overactive thyroid who likes to bang things and throw things around."

"I don't care what he's called," Jojo exclaimed. "I know what I saw—and felt—last night. So did everyone else. That book didn't have a jet engine inside. Something tore it out of my hand and flung it around. And that something adds up to the guy I was reading about. Take it or leave it." Jojo was adamant. "I'm going to try and contact this character when we get back. I'll bet he's got a treasure buried somewhere."

"Jojo," said Jennifer, "the trouble with you is that you believe everything you read. You're so far out, you're unreal."

Jojo scowled at his older sister. "Boy," he said, "I hope Sweeney or whoever it is gives you the business!"

"I'm with you, Jojo," Sarilee added.

"O.K. kids, that's enough," Millie interrupted. "Let's not get hysterical. Anyone hungry? It's lunchtime."

Sweeney had kept to himself while the Framers alternately swam and sunbathed. He went along on the ride to the beach out of idle curiosity. And he returned with them soon after lunch.

Not even when Les pulled up at a string of broken-down souvenir stands on the way back to Limeshade Villa, did Sweeney bother anyone. He did not feel compelled to annoy the living outside of his own bailiwick—Limeshade Villa. It was not that the idea never occurred to him. Halfway through the picnic lunch, Sweeney decided to heave a coconut or two at the Framers. He climbed one of the gracefully sloping palms but could not wrench loose a single coconut. He wrestled with the coconuts with ever-increasing anger and frustration, not to mention every ounce of superghostly strength he could muster. The coconuts would not budge and Sweeney gave up. It was as if the pi-

rate was powerless. This was not a totally surprising condition since most poltergeists were, traditionally, at their noisy, pesty best in situations that required their special talents. This situation—the lovely beach, the sunny day, the pleasant family picnic, the grand Caribbean horizon—was not one of those special places or moments. Sweeney would bide his time.

In any event, *Sweeney followed* Millie and the kids around as they picked over straw baskets and boxes, varnished conch shells and polished wood sea gulls. Les thought that this particular souvenir-hunting stop was a waste of time and refused to get out of the car. In a way, he was right. No one bought anything. They continued on their way back to the house.

Les brought the auto to a sudden stop halfway up the driveway. Martin Martin's donkey, George, stood squarely in the middle. Coraleen was desperately trying to push him back and head him toward the rear of the carport. Les had slammed the brakes so hard that *Sweeney fell off the roof of the car.*

"'Ere now, you dumb beast," he snapped, *"look what you've done. Oi'll teach you a thing or two!"*

Sweeney picked himself up, waved his cutlass and made for the animal. Les stuck his head out the car window. "Where is Martin?" he asked. "I wish I knew," Coraleen replied. "He hasn't been here all day."

Suddenly, George snorted and pawed the ground.

"Look out, Coraleen!"

72

Coraleen backed away.

George bucked then kicked his hind legs straight out. He could not see Sweeney, but he could smell him with the extra sensory perception that animals sometimes have. *Sweeney moved in.* George backed up. *Sweeney whipped his cutlass within an inch of George's nose.* There was terror in George's eyes. He was not going to wait in that driveway to see what would happen next. With one great "hee-haw" the donkey hurdled the cement wall and disappeared down the road.

"Good riddance," Sweeney yelled after him.

"Everyone out," bawled Les. "Last stop! Haunted Villa! House of the poltergeist! Sweeney's hideaway!"

"I don't think that's funny, Les," Millie sniffed.

"Well, something made that animal take off. Did you see the look in his eyes? Donkeys aren't known for their track records."

"Maybe so. But we are supposed to be here to relax. So far we've been here four days and I'm still a nervous wreck."

"Cheer up, honey. There are still four days to go. Besides, what's a vacation without a little mystery to liven things up? I'll tell you what. The afternoon is still young. Let's clean up, go into Ocho Rios, spend some time around Pineapple Place, take a drive up that tropical canyon—what's it called? —Fern Gully, that's it—we missed it the last time—and then dine out in style at the Tower Isle. Is that battle plan O.K. with everyone?"

It was. Coraleen, still dumfounded over the burro's behavior, was given the rest of the day off. An hour later, a buoyant bunch of Framers headed for Ocho Rios.

So did Sweeney. Only this time he straddled the hood of the car. And from deep down inside his billowing coat he dredged up a large telescope with which to survey the road and scenes ahead.

A billion stars crowded the clear deep sky when the Framers finally returned to Limeshade Villa. The moon was bright. The air was dry and balmy. It had been a long day.

"We were lucky to be seated for dinner, Les," Millie said, sighing.

"I know, the place was jammed. Next time I'll make a reservation."

"All's well that ends well. Everything was delicious."

"It was very embarrassing."

"For who, Jenny, old girl," Sarilee snapped, "you or our poor waiter? What do you suppose happened to him anyway? I thought all those lobsters were coming straight at me when he fell."

"Gad," Millie added, "what a mess! The whole place was covered with lobsters and goo."

"Gross," was all that Sarilee could say to punctuate her own remarks.

"Strange that no one was hit," Les observed.

"Sweeney! That's what happened to him," Jojo piped up. "Sweeney! He tripped up that guy. I'll bet anything that Sweeney goes where we go."

"That's right, laddie. Sweeney. Oi put me foot in 'is way. Cooooo. What a mess. Oi 'ad better luck wi' that one than wi' the coconuts."

"Nonsense, Jojo," replied his mother. "I think we had all better go to bed before our ghostitis get any worse."

"Not until I knock on a few walls. Maybe he'll answer."

Jojo began rapping and listening. Sarilee joined him. Millie, Les, and Jennifer went to bed.

"Sweeney. Mister Sweeney," they tentatively called. "Are you there?"

No one answered. Sweeney kept his silence. It was a long day for him too. Besides, he had other plans—some rapping of his own—later. He did not want to become too friendly with the American family that intruded upon his domain.

"What was that?"

"Relax, Millie," said Les soothingly. "It's Jojo. He's still knocking things trying to get a rise out of Sweeney."

"There you go again. Sweeney. Ghosts. Poltergeists. Have you any idea what time it is. It's two in the morning. Tell Jojo to get back into bed—now—immediately."

"Jojo," Les called. "Enough! You'd better get some sleep."

The rapping continued—faster and louder.

"I hear you, Dad. I am in bed and I'm not knocking."

"Then who is?"

"Guess who?" Jennifer and Sarilee both screamed.

"Sweeney?"

"Something like that."

"You got it right the first time," Jojo insisted. "Sweeney."

"For heaven's sake, Les, that knocking is all around us and

it's getting louder—and closer. Good Lord It's here in the bedroom! Do something!"

"What do you want me to do?"

"Something! Anything! You're always telling us what a war hero you were."

Millie pulled the covers over her head.

Les jumped out of bed and scrambled around the room banging his fists on the walls. Jennifer, Sarilee, and Jojo stood in the bedroom doorway watching their father frantically pound the walls until he collapsed on the bed, exhausted. The silence that followed was stunning.

Sweeney had quit his rapping too. He could not stand the thunderous racket created by Les Framer and retreated to his seat on top of the bar to decide his next assault.

"Hey. How about that? I got rid of the creature." Still no one moved, fully expecting the ghostly noises to return. They didn't. Not right away, anyway. *Sweeney let the Framers disperse, each to his own bed.*

Sweeney waited about fifteen minutes more just to assure himself that all the Framers were comfortable again. Assured that they were, he marched to the front door, walked right through it, turned and with a dramatic flourish slammed the brass door knocker a few times.

"It's back, Les, It's back. Oh my God!" Millie whispered.

"I hear it. It's at the front door. Just ignore it."

Les slowly crawled out of bed. "Where are you going?" Millie asked.

"Don't worry, honey, I'm not going to open it. I'm just going to look in on the kids."

"I'm going with you," Millie decided.

The two of them tiptoed to the other side of the house as *Sweeney continued to slam the knocker.* They found their offspring with the covers pulled tightly over their heads. No one was about to find out who might or might not be on the other side of the front door. Millie and Les returned to their own bedroom and pulled the covers over their heads. *Sweeney, disgusted with his inability to thoroughly terrorize the Framers, finally gave up and let the night pass.*

WEDNESDAY
February 23, 1972

The Framer kids slept well after having stayed awake as long as they could discussing the night's strange excitement.

Les and Millie slept reasonably well after the noisy ordeal. Les, too, would have slept very well if his skittish wife had not stayed awake—or rather half awake—most of the time, insisting that he investigate every creak, groan, and chirp

that filled the natural Jamaican night.

"Comes the morning, Les," Millie kept groggily reminding her equally groggy spouse, "we are packing and getting out of here. I'm not going to spend another day in this madhouse!"

"Where'll we go? We can't go home yet. Our plane leaves on Saturday. I have already reconfirmed our return reservations. Besides we have already paid for this place."

"You paid for it. Not me. We'll go to the Tower Isle, that's where! They've got real people over there, lots of them."

"Fine," Les replied. "They are all booked up. No rooms. And we can't afford it anyway."

"Then we'll sleep in the lobby. We'll have a sleep-in—a protest against male chauvinist ghosts."

"Why don't you try and get some sleep, dear. I think Sweeney has gone away. We'll talk about it in the morning."

Millie finally fell asleep—more or less unconscious from nervous exhaustion. Les was grateful. *Sweeney, too, was quiet.*

By midmorning everyone was awake arguing over the merits of staying or leaving before the sun set on another Limeshade Villa day.

Sarilee and Jojo were for staying. They wanted the adventure. They wanted to know what would happen next. And they both silently thought of the amazing story they would tell to the rest of Aspetuck when they got home. Their names might be in the newspapers. Jojo, for that matter, was beginning to plan a sixth- and seventh-grade lecture tour.

Even Jennifer was caught up in the general excitement—losing her studied cool, as it were. She was determined to see it through for no other reason than to face the challenge this "thing" offered—a challenge that tested her will to survive and win (whatever it was one was supposed to win in a natural-supernatural confrontation).

Les cast his lot with that of his children, but for different reasons. For one thing, this vacation was expensive enough. He did not want to go broke in the process, a condition that could result by a move to the nearest resort hotel. Most of all, he could not cope with the idea of packing and unpacking again, of leaving Limeshade Villa for another Jamaican spot. He came to Limeshade Villa for a week or so and here he intended to stay until it was time to go home.

"Sweeney is finished," Les proclaimed. "He's finished because he could not scare us off. Now let's get some sun."

"Right on, Dad."

Only Millie had misgivings. Only Millie felt the continuing threat to their peace of mind. And as always, Millie was ready to travel. Anywhere would do. It did not matter. But Millie was outvoted. She agreed, however reluctantly, to give Limeshade Villa another twenty-four-hour try.

Coraleen, who was on the job as usual, had no misgivings at

all. Although still puzzled over Martin Martin's failure to make an appearance yesterday and again this morning, blaming his absence on a more substantial earthly reason—a bottle or two of Charlie's rum—she now was convinced that the Framers were, indeed, out of their American minds.

"That's what happens to people who have too much of everything," she philosophized to no one in particular.

Only Sweeney heard the remark. "Cooooo, love," he whispered. "You don't know the 'alf of hit."

"Too much money," Coraleen continued, "too much responsibility, too much snow, too much worry, too much food, too much booze, too much television, too much of everything. It's no wonder they need a vacation."

However sympathetic Coraleen Morgan seemed to be, she quickly returned to her own connection with these strangers who came out of the sky on Saturday last and who will depart the same way on Saturday next. "And it's only Wednesday, mon," she groaned.

Sweeney bothered no one. He spent the morning, noon, and night reclining, comfortably, on a chaise longue, not too many feet from the apron of the Limeshade Villa swimming pool. There he evoked a tangle of memories of his former natural life.

"Hif that young laddie wants to find Spanish coin," Sweeney *mumbled to himself, "'E'll not foind them around these parts. 'E'll 'ave to go to the Palisadoe, to old Port Royal, and jump into the bay. That's where me 'eart is. That's where me old city is—at the bottom. There's a mountain of silver down there. Cooooo. Hif Oi 'ad hit to do over again; if Oi 'ad me youth again, that's where Oi'd go—to old Port Royal."*

Sweeney was confused—dreaming and boasting as well.

He could not have remembered old Port Royal, the thriving pirate capital of the world, in all of its wicked glory. Once situated at the end of a crooked thread of land that undulated like a snake from the mainland—from what is now the city of Kingston on the southeast coast—old Port Royal slid hissing into a foaming sea during a violent earthquake. And with it went some two thousand buildings, about two thousand people, and most of the plunder they had collected over too many years from the hapless victims both on sea and on land. It was as if the Almighty pointed his thunderbolt of retribution upon the rum-soaked Sodom and Gomorrah of the Caribbean and in one unmeasurable instant of time destroyed the worst unreconstructed sinners in this part of His world.

That was in 1692. Sweeney, not yet a man, was only seven years old. A proficient pickpocket on the London wharves,

88

he was fast showing signs of his later self. By the time he became a well-muscled seagoing robber, old Port Royal was a legendary place in a watery grave. Pieces of the city remained standing. But soon after a fire destroyed most of those. A new Port Royal was built and Kingston, across the harbor, began to stir with an ever-increasing beat of life.

Sweeney knew where the old city lay. He knew, too, the immensity of the stolen fortunes that rested on the bottom. So did everyone else who sailed those waters. But old Port Royal was beyond their reach. As for Sweeney, he could not dive that deeply in his youth and never tried. Neither did anyone else at the time. The only thing Port Royal ever did for Sweeney was to hang him at Gallows Point.

"Oh, me poor neck," he muttered every so often whenever the memory of Gallows Point pierced his ghostly consciousness. "But Oi fooled them, Oi did," he would counter with a certain smug pride. "Oi may be not among the living, but Oi'm still kicking, Oi ham."

All the time Sweeney whiled away on the chaise longue, his recollections danced from one mean adventure to the other. One such vivid incident occurred off the coast of Florida when he was at the height of his reputation. There, he and his cutthroats took a well-armed Spanish freighter loaded with silver and wine. So heavy in the water was the Spaniard that Sweeney was upon her like a leopard on a chicken. Sweeney put the terror-struck crew off on a God-forsaken treeless Bahamian sandbar without food, water, shelter, or weapons. He burned their ship to the waterline before their very eyes and used the hulk for target practice until every splinter disappeared forever. He sailed a short distance away, divided the booty among his own men and pro-

ceeded to let certain hands drink themselves into a stupor on Spanish wine in full view of the unfortunate Spaniards. Drunk himself, Sweeney then relieved these men—those he no longer trusted—about a dozen in all—of the swag he had just doled out and with the approval of those more loyal and less sotted shoved each of them into the water like rag dolls. There they quickly drowned.

The Spaniards were horrified. But Sweeney was not finished. He weighed anchor and approached the sandbar. He remained at this station overnight to allow the Spaniards time to contemplate their fate. In the morning, Sweeney trained his guns on the sandbar and the quaking Spaniards dropped to their knees. But not a shot was fired. Instead, Sweeney dispatched a boat with an offer.

"Hif any of you devils want to live to see your wives and mothers, ye'll come aboard and sail wi' me."

About fifteen of them scrambled into the boat and were taken aboard. The rest—about 20 men including the captain and mates—stubbornly refused. They were left on the sandbar to die. However, fortunately for them, they lived to tell the tale. A luckier Spanish vessel rescued them, half crazy, several days later.

Regardless of his brutality, Sweeney, from time to time, showed a compassionate side to his nature. He kept recalling to himself at the poolside the several days he tracked a sloop off the Carolinas trying to make up his mind whether or not it was worth the effort to overtake her. Finally, he did. What he found was a slaver out of the West Indies bound for a Carolina marketplace. Sweeney's rage was awesome. He detested slavers from the day he first sailed

*aboard one as a ship's boy. And that rage seethed within
him from that moment on. Slavers were filthy—filthy with
the dirt of their miserable human cargo chained like animals below—filthy with the garbage of their unkempt crews
—filthy with the surliness of the traders who ran them.*

"Filthy, filthy, filthy," he bellowed.

*Sweeney trafficked in many things and wrote his own set of
terror-filled laws. Most of this was aimed at the Spanish. It
was the custom of the time for men of his classless breed.
But there was one thing he could not stomach—the buying
and selling of human beings. The shackles of slavery were
an abomination beyond the worst crimes he could commit.*

*"Everyone, black or green," he muttered, "'as the roight to
live or die by 'is own services, by 'is own wits, loose and
free, not at the end of a chain loike a dog."*

"But Oi fixed them, Oi did."

*And Sweeney, the ghost of Limeshade Villa, went on to re-
call with some amusement how he forced the traders to
clean up their foul ship "until it shone loike a broight dia-
mond"; how he freed the suffering blacks and chained up
the traders in their places; how he put aboard several of his
own men; how he took on a number of the blacks who insisted on repaying him by sailing with him as pirates; and
finally, how he turned the glistening slaver around with the
white traders chained below and the blacks free above and
headed her back to where she came from.*

"Oi'm not so bad after all," he decided.

Sweeney took great pleasure in comparing himself to the vilest creature it was ever his misfortune to know—Edward Teach—Blackbeard. The plain fact was that the only real thing they had in common was their blackbeards. And even there, there was a noticeable, if minor, difference. Sweeney's beard was a well-manicured explosion of thick hair. Teach's beard, on the other hand, was a long collection of curls tied in various places with ribbons.

"'E taught me all Oi knew," Sweeney remembered. "'E was the devil himself."

Sweeney sailed with Blackbeard as a teen-ager. He learned his trade so well that Blackbeard made him the captain of a small French ship that attacked him and lost in a furious encounter off the West African Coast. Sweeney was only twenty and Blackbeard was an unknown privateer who had not yet decided to terrorize the Carolina and Virginia waters. But instead of putting in with Teach, Sweeney went into business for himself. Blackbeard vowed that if he ever caught up with Sweeney again he'd cut off his ears, pickle his tongue, and bury him alive.

That day almost came eleven years later. Sweeney was a wanted man by then.

"Cooooo. Oi thought Oi'd bought hit," Sweeney croaked.

The two pirates, Blackbeard and Sweeney, stalked each other for days on a gently rolling sea, not too far from Ocracoke Inlet, North Carolina, Blackbeard's home base. Neither of them knew who the other was. Each of them thought the other to be a Spanish merchantman. Both decided to attack the other at the same time. Both ships converged, struck *their Spanish ensigns, hoisted their black flags, and cannonaded each other at will. It was too late to stop.*

Sweeney had no trouble recognizing Teach, who stood on the quarterdeck, laden with pistols and knives, two burning twisted hemp cords protruding from under his misshapen hat on both sides of his head like a pair of fiery horns. Blackbeard had no idea who his adversary was except that he looked a good deal like himself. Sweeney would have liked to have killed Teach if he could now that he recognized him. Teach, however, enjoyed the battle as pure sport since this was a fight for pirate supremacy, now that it had begun.

Sweeney was annihilated. He lost his ship, his entire crew, and whatever booty he had on board. Blackbeard fished him out of the water and congratulated him for his fierce courage.

"What's your name, you bloody devil?"

"Philips. William Philips," Sweeney replied. He was not about to reveal himself before this monstrous seadog.

Blackbeard took him before Charles Eden, the governor of North Carolina. Still unrecognized, Sweeney was easily drawn into a pact with the crooked governor; a pact that Blackbeard also enjoyed; a pact that allowed Blackbeard to ravage the shipping along the Carolina coast. In return for one half of any booty, Sweeney, alias Philips, would take, Blackbeard resolved to do him no further harm and the governor would give him a vessel and a crew of his own choice. Not only that, the governor would give him a formal commission placing Sweeney, alias Philips, under his protection.

Thus Sweeney, having agreed to all this, became an officer on a privateer owned by the governor in league with Blackbeard but operating for the King of England. Of course the King knew nothing about this.

"Oi found me a stout crew. Some of them knew oo Oi was. Oi swore them to secrecy. They enjoyed the trick on poor old Teach. They gave me a foine ship, too, just as they said they would. And on the morning toide we ran for New York. Oi never saw the governor or Teach again. Poor old Teach. 'E soon bought hit."

News of Teach's death spread like a hurricane from Boston to Spanish Town, Jamaica's capital. No one ever thought such a thing possible, as if Blackbeard was an eternal demon. On November 21, 1718, some two years after the Blackbeard-Sweeney battle, Teach was caught at the mouth of the Ocracoke Inlet and violently slain by Lieutenant Robert Maynard of the British man-of-war Pearl. Lieutenant Maynard was dispatched for that sole purpose following a proclamation issued by Alexander Spotswood, the governor of Virginia. The proclamation read in part:

It is, amongst other things enacted, that all and every person or persons, who from and after the 14th day of November, in the year of Our Lord 1718, and before the 14th day of November, in the year of Our Lord 1719, shall take any Pirate or Pirates, between the degrees of 34 and 39 Northern latitude, and within 100 leagues of the Continent of Virginia, or within the Provinces of Virginia, or North Carolina, upon the conviction, or making due proof of the killing of all, and every such Pirate, and Pirates, before the Governor and Council, shall be entitled to have, and receive out of the public money, in the hands of the Treasurer of this Colony, the several rewards following; that is to say, for Edward

Teach, commonly called Captain Teach or Blackbeard, 100 pounds . . . etc.

Teach's head was hung from the bowsprit of Lieutenant Maynard's ship. Those of his crew still alive following the assault were hanged; all, that is, save two. One was pardoned a hopeless cripple, mangled by Blackbeard himself. The other was acquitted for some unaccountable reason that history fails to mention. As for Teach's partner in crime, Governor Charles Eden of North Carolina and some of his official underlings who were also partners in the conspiracy, no one ever linked them with the atrocities for which Teach paid with his head. In fact, Governor Eden went on governing until 1722.

Day became night. Night became dawn. *Sweeney bothered no one. The old pirate was lost in time, in another dimension. He had too much to remember.*

THURSDAY
February 24, 1972

"You see. What did I tell you," Les Framer proclaimed to everyone. "Not a sound all day yesterday. Not a sound all night last night. Not a knock. Not a rap. Not a tap. I told you we were too much for that poltergeist!"

"Sweeney, Dad," said Jojo with a hint of disappointment.

"Ghost," said Sarilee and Jennifer in unison.

"Duppy," Coraleen insisted. This was Jamaica. The least these people could do was to learn to speak like a Jamaican.

"Duppy!" Sweeney exclaimed with annoyance. "Hit sounds more loike a fish than the spook Oi ham."

"Thing," said Millie sarcastically.

"All right, have it your own way. But let's knock it off for a while," Les demanded. "He's gone, Millie. Whatever it was is gone. So leave it be and relax everybody."

"So is Martin Martin gone, Les. He hasn't been seen around here since Tuesday. His donkey is back though. Who knows, maybe Martin is the rapper."

Les ignored her.

"O.K. Here's the schedule for the day. Take it or leave it. As of now we are going to the market. Right Coraleen?"

"Right, sir, mon."

"When we return we'll take a dip in the pool, have some lunch, sleep it off, and take another dip. Then we'll go see that place at Discovery Bay where Columbus landed on one of his voyages. Then we'll come back here, work a little more on our tans, have dinner, dress up and catch the show at the Tower Isle. You know, limbo dancers, calypso and all that." Les was making an effort to recapture the romance of their short holiday.

"Take me to my leader," Jennifer groaned with her former air of contrived boredom.

"Say, that's right, Les," Millie suddenly decided, "since when have you appointed yourself my leader?"

"It's very simple. If we do not go marketing now, we may

not eat cheaply tonight, tomorrow, and maybe Saturday morning. Right Coraleen?"

"Right, sir, mon."

"Now if none of you want to go to Discovery Bay, that's fine with me. If you'd rather go rafting on the Rio Grande like we did the last time, that, too, would be fine. I'll go any-where you want to go. But if you, Millie, want to stay home alone tonight and run the risk of a return engagement of the ghost that runs this place, that, too, is fine with me. Just re-member no one will be around to hear your screams. I am going out to the car."

"We're with you, Dad."

"So ham Oi, Governor."

They all followed quickly after him, *Sweeney included.* Les started the car and turned to Millie with a bemused smirk on his face. "Now you know who your leader is."

"Oi ham," said Sweeney whipping out his telescope as he settled himself on the hood of the car.

"Male chauvinist," she retorted.

Thursday was nearing midnight. Limeshade Villa was dark, quiet and not at all foreboding. Its occupants—that is, all but one—lay asleep in their beds, disturbed perhaps by random fleeting dreams.

Coraleen did the marketing with Millie at her side watching the budget. The rest of the Framers followed them from store to shop like a line of ducklings.

Sweeney peered at them marching around from his post on the hood of the car. From time to time he would train his telescope on them whenever they seemed to get out of range. It was almost as if he did not want to be left alone. Other than that he hardly moved. There was no real adventure in any of this for him. He was bored.

Following a swim at the pool and lunch, the Framers *and Sweeney* took to the road again. *The irrepressible pirate went along to do whatever mischief crossed his mind. The only success he had any distance from Limeshade Villa was tripping up the waiter at the Tower Isle dining room. Beyond that he had tried in vain to wrench a coconut loose from a tree. That was on Tuesday. But he was powerless, or seemed to be, on that particular occasion.*

In any event, while Millie, Les, Jennifer, Sarilee and Jojo dallied among the stalls and marts of Pineapple Place,

102

Sweeney nervously clung to the car. He was so bewildered by the roar of the traffic and the jostling confusion of people that jammed Pineapple Place, he could not do a mischievous thing, let alone try.

As the powerful crescendo of the twentieth century came at him from every direction, Sweeney yearned for the windy space of the sea—his lawless sea—whatever the risk. Once during the tortured clatter of the afternoon, Sweeney thought about sliding back into his grave to get away from it all. Yet, he resisted the temptation. He was not ready for that! He would never be ready for that again! Haunting the Framers, as new and unsuccessful as he was at it, might be a poor substitute for a wild life on the high seas, but since he was on dry land, it was better than nothing. Besides, how else could he drive them away?

Underneath it all, there were two things Sweeney refused to admit to himself: he was older than he seemed able to comprehend—nearly three centuries old—and, in a manner of speaking, he was only a shadow of his former self. More to the point, the ancient pirate had mellowed more than he realized. He had more pride than punch. He was not half as ferocious as he seemed to think. Moreover, he was losing his zest for haunting people who would not be haunted; who would not be absolutely paralyzed with fear of him—not that he would give up his capers entirely.

"These simple fools," he said with the faint hint of a whimper, "think Oi'm a joke. Well, has soon has Oi get me bearings, the joke will be on them. Oi'll spook them good, Oi will."

For the moment anyway, Sweeney kept a watchful eye on

the horn-blasting twentieth century, twisting and turning with the vibrating roar of it all. In the meanwhile, Millie had treated herself to a handsomely embroidered straw beach basket. Jojo insisted on having a straw hat and Les insisted they all have straw hats. By the time they were ready to leave, everyone wore a straw with orange bands upon which was printed "Jamaica, Jamaica, Jamaica," around and around and around.

"Now we look like tourists," Jennifer complained.

Les finished off their modest purchase by ordering some fine native liqueurs which he would have to pick up at a special duty-free counter at the airport on Saturday.

Sweeney was quite relieved when the Framers piled back into their rented car and left the shattering noises behind.

They drove westward past Dunn's River Falls; past some burning sugar-cane fields; through the busy town of St. Ann's Bay; past the site of the early Spanish village of Sevilla Nueva; and finally reached Discovery Bay, about midway on the highway that stretched along the north coast from Mo Bay in the west to Port Antonio in the east.

There on a small promontory park overlooking the endless blue-green sea they found a tablet telling them that Columbus landed in this vicinity in May, 1494.

104

Jojo, always well informed about such things, supplied his family with a few missing but basic facts. He told how Columbus returned some years later with his son, Diego, and left Diego to colonize the island for Spain. The first thing on the younger Columbus' list of things to do was to get rid of the Arawak Indians, the original inhabitants of the island. Today, there are no Arawaks because Diego and those Spanish Conquistadores who followed him to the island murdered them all. The English grabbed the island about 150 years later bringing piracy, and eventually black slavery, to Jamaica.

With that bit of history under their belts, thanks to Jojo's reading thirst, the Framers returned to Limeshade Villa for dinner and the late evening limbo show at the Tower Isle Hotel.

Even Sweeney was captivated by the tour. It was not the Jamaica he knew or expected to see. But so intrigued was the old ghost that he forgot any mischief making he had in mind.

"Ladies and Gentlemen," said the master of ceremonies in his soft, precise, nasal twang that was more British than Britain herself. "Ladies and Gentlemen," he repeated, "I should like at this time to introduce to you one of the world's greatest performers. Formerly a center ring entertainer with the renown Ringling Brothers and Barnum & Bailey Circus in America, currently on a Caribbean tour and soon to be seen at the Lido on the Champs-Elysees in Gay Paree," here the M.C. gave what he figured to be a naughty wink that suited his reference to Paris, "I give you Pierre Boolevard, a French wonder."

With a sweep of his arm, out stepped Pierre Boolevard who was neither French nor Pierre Boolevard, but an Austrian sword swallower named Rudi Wolffburg. Arriving on stage with Rudi, who, incidentally, gave the impression of having been carved out of rock, was a rack of swords, tubes, and torches pushed by a twinkling, bikini-clad show girl, whom he introduced as his daughter.

Rudi immediately grasped one of the slender swords, showed it to the audience, flexed it once or twice and then shoved it down his throat, wasting no time in pulling it out.

From that moment on Rudi Wolffburg would never be the same again. *Sweeney decided to get into the act.*

Rudi chose another sword. As he was about to plunge it downward into his throat, *Sweeney grabbed his wrist in an iron, bone-crushing grip.* No matter how hard the sword

106

swallower tried to break free, he succeeded only in making the audience laugh hysterically. The scene repeated itself over and over again with different swords. *Sweeney held fast. It was a test of wills and Sweeney won. He had humiliated Rudi Wolffburg, the great Pierre Boolevard.* The audience, unaware of the ghost's presence, thought it was a great comic act. They shrieked, stomped, and applauded their approval. The sword swallower thought otherwise. In one final dispirited happening he broke all of his swords across his knee and fainted. His assistant fled. Everyone cheered figuring this was part of the act, too. And finally, they gave him a standing ovation when a couple of waiters dragged him out of sight. The audience went wild. *Sweeney was pleased with himself.*

No one, not even the Framers, suspected the cause of the sword swallower's problem was a spirit named Sweeney. Only Pierre Boolevard—the great Pierre Boolevard—felt the cold metallic grip on his wrist. And he wasn't talking. He couldn't. He was scared speechless.

"What a finish!" Sarilee screamed along with the rest of the audience.

"Sit down!" her mother ordered.

"Boy! Those swords must cost a fortune if he keeps breaking them all the time," Les mused.

"Nonsense," replied Jojo, "they're props, fake swords. I bet he puts them back together again in his dressing room."

"Cool," was Jennifer's one word comment.

108

"Ye're all daft," Sweeney answered.

"Ladies and Gentlemen." The master of ceremonies was back on the stage again, surprised but delighted with Rudi Wolffburg's off beat, unscheduled performance. "Ladies and Gentlemen, the Tower Isle management is pleased to present for your enjoyment the finest limbo troupe in Jamaica —the Black River Dancers."

A dozen colorfully dressed dancers rushed onstage to the steady beat of the bongo drums. As several hotel workers arranged a bamboo pole on two upright supports, the troupe—men and women alike—gyrated their slack bodies to the wildly gay and melodic rhythm of a calypso band.

Sweeney, caught in the middle of planning his next test of power, could not sit still. He jumped up, joined the troupe and did some fast stepping, kicking, and whirling routines of his own.

"Cooooo. This his the loife. Oi always loiked to do a jig or two. Oi'm a bit rusty but hits in me blood." And Sweeney went right on cavorting to the native rhythms even when half the dancers were encouraging any one of their number to snake and slide under the constantly lowered bamboo pole without touching it. None of them did. And at times the pole could not have been more than a few inches off the floor.

Sweeney paid no attention to any of this. As long as the music continued, he danced. When finally the entertainment ended, Sweeney vowed he'd come back, but not without brushing up on his "jigging," as he put it.

"Les. Are you awake? Les. I heard something. Who's there? Les. Wake up."

"Wh-Wha-What's going on. What's the matter? Who's where? What's there? For Pete's sake, Millie, I just birdied the ninth hole at Aspetuck for the first time in my life and you had to wake me up before I could enjoy it."

"Something's walking around out there."

"It's just the kids. See. Here they are. Hey, what are you kids doing in here in the middle of the night?"

"Do you mind, Dad? We heard something rattling around near the bar—we think—and it's giving us the creeps. If it's all the same to you two, we'd like to stay with you for a while."

"I didn't hear anything."

"You never hear anything when you don't want to. The other ni—"

"There it goes again, Dad."

"I hear it. Some racket."

"What are you going to do, Les, just listen? Aren't you going to have a look?"

110

Les moved toward the bedroom door—slowly. Millie and the kids ganged up close behind. "Don't push," he cautioned. Les tiptoed beyond the door where he had a better view of the living room and dining area.

There, at the other end, bathed in the cool blue light of the moon was the bar, jerking and rocking back and forth as if something or someone was pounding it. *And indeed there was someone—Sweeney—dancing and jigging on top for all he was worth.*

"It's back?" Millie whispered.

"It's back," Les answered. "Come see for yourselves."

They did, crowding around Les and clinging to one another as they took in the incredible performance of the bar.

"'Ow's that ducks. Oi'm getting sharper hall the toime."

Sweeney was not addressing the Framers. He did not even see them as he continued his stomping. And if he did, he showed no interest. Instead, he was displaying his fancy footwork for an unseen guest. Sweeney had a late date—an admiring ladyfriend from out of his distant past. Keeping time at the bar, rhythmically whacking it with her trusty battle-ax, was Anne Bonny.

Anne Bonny, that notorious lady buccaneer who struck her own brand of fear into the hearts of stout sailors, had returned. She and Sweeney jigged the night through with wild abandon. It was not until daybreak that the house quit rocking and the dust settled—and the Framers collapsed in their beds.

FRIDAY
February 25, 1972

"Holy smokes! What a night! I thought the house would fall apart. Fantastic! Who will ever believe us when we tell them about this vacation? Even Coraleen doesn't believe us. She thinks we're still trying to put her on or something."

"Maybe we ought to get Coraleen to spend the night with us, Jojo, so she can see for herself," Sarilee replied.

"Yea," Jojo added, "and nothing would happen. Besides, she's still too mad over Mr. Martin's disappearance to take us seriously. He's left her with a lot of chores. I'll bet you anything that Sweeney—and I just know it's that pirate—he's probably buried under the house somewhere—had something to do with the old guy taking off."

Jojo and Sarilee were sitting at the edge of the pool dangling their feet in the warm water. It was late morning. They were waiting for the rest of the family to stir. This was their last full day on the island.

Sweeney was sprawled under a stunted palm tree, trying to nap with one eye on Sarilee and Jojo. He was all in from his night's frolic.

"'E's a smart one, that laddie is," Sweeney muttered as he half listened to their conversation. "But if anyone thinks Oi'm going to tell them Oi'm me, they're balmy. Oi've got to be careful. Oi've got to keep me hindependence. Keep them guessing, Oi always say. If Oi lose the upper 'and, Oi'll never 'aunt anybody. Oi'll 'ave to crawl back into me grave and stay there—soilent forever. Oi 'aven't a moind to do that!"

"What makes you so sure it was Sweeney, Jojo?"

"Well, the more I read about him and his hanging, the weirder this whole thing becomes. Even Dad thinks it's Sweeney. He thinks like me, you know. Anyway, there's no sense to it. It sounds crazy. But has anyone come up with a better idea? A more exciting idea? Fantastic! Wait'll we get home. I'm going to do a lot of research on ghosts, spirits, and poltergeists. I've heard of this sort of thing happening before. But I always figured the people to be weirdos. Now I'm not sure they were. We're not weirdos, are we?"

114

"Nope. I don't think so. At least I'm not. Sometimes I have my doubts about the rest of you."

"You're a real big deal, aren't you," Jojo retorted as he pushed his sister into the water, falling in himself. They did not hear the distant voices drifting from their parents' bedroom as they splashed around.

Neither did Sweeney. He was fast asleep for the first time since last Sunday.

116

"Not another minute, Les. Not another minute. Not another night in this house. I've had it. We are packing and cutting out! Now!"

"Now hold on a second, honey. Let's think this thing out. First of all we don't have to leave right away. Nothing happens around here of any consequence during the daytime. If anything, we'll spend the whole day down at the beach. Second of all we've got just enough money to get us home tomorrow and not a dime left to put the five of us up in a hotel for the night."

"What about using your credit cards?"

"I didn't bring them. Remember? We decided to pay cash for everything. We didn't want to face any bills later. Remember?

"And I'll tell you another thing. There isn't a vacant room at any of the hotels from here to Mo Bay. And I'm not about to go to Kingston either."

"There must be something. Tell them it's an emergency."

"What emergency?"

"Ghosts. Anything."

"That's crazy."

"Then we'll go to Mo Bay and spend the night at the airport."

"That's crazier! I'd rather sleep here than on my suitcase or a hard bench. But I'll tell you what. We'll compromise. I'll meet you halfway. We'll all spend the day at the beach. It's going to be a hot and gorgeous day—our last."

"Maybe our last for all time," Millie interrupted sarcastically.

Les went on. "We'll picnic down there, come back for dinner, and make an attempt to sleep here tonight. In the meantime we'll be all packed and ready to go. At the first sign and sound of Sweeney, if he as much as makes a knock—no matter what time of night—we'll leave—God only knows where."

"To Mo Bay and the airport."

"O.K. To Mo Bay and the airport. Is it a deal?"

"It's a deal, Les," Millie finally agreed. She was resigned to whatever fate awaited them for she knew deep down that they would remain one more night at Limeshade Villa no matter how many times Sweeney knocked.

"I really think we ought to stay." Jennifer had been awake for the past ten minutes and now sauntered into the bedroom to add her opinion. "Things are warming up around here. We've come this far. We don't want to miss anything."

118

Millie glared at her oldest daughter who was casually leaning in the doorway. "And I suppose you want to find out what else is in store for us."

"Why not? This is one of those once-in-a-lifetime things. Isn't it?"

"Good grief!" Millie snapped, "aren't you the brave one. Don't forget, young lady, it was you, your sister, and your brother who spent half the night in here with us—not vice versa."

"O.K. you two. Save your energy for the beach. Let's have some breakfast."

There were a few people scattered along the crescent-shaped beach when the Framers arrived. That alone made Millie feel much better. She felt a little less trapped, a little less cornered at the sight of them. The sand was warm and spotless, washed clean by the outgoing tide. It was like a soft, smooth, shapelessly rippled carpet. It was the kind of creamy sand to snuggle against or to wiggle one's toes into.

As the day slowly wore on, it became more difficult for the Framers to recall the chaos of last night. The more sun and water they soaked up the more they shed every vestige of anxiety they had brought to the beach with them. And by the time the lazy sun began to slowly drop from the sky, they were soothed beyond care. Tomorrow seemed so far away.

"Why do we have to hang around here the rest of the evening?" Sarilee wanted to know. "This is our last night. Let's do something."

"Aye, ducks, let's do something," Sweeney chimed in. "Oi've no wish to 'ang around 'ere or anywhere," he added,

rubbing his throat and the back of his neck. The pirate spirit had spent the last hour sitting on the bar, cross-legged as usual, watching the Framers dine. He was cheered by the prospect that the family would soon be on their way out of the house for good. Tomorrow was not approaching fast enough to suit him.

"Fine idea," Millie agreed jumping up from the table. She had been having second thoughts about the darkening night. The more time she had to spend away from Lime-shade Villa, now, the better. "But first we'll get organized and do a little packing. One strange noise and I want to be ready to leave."

Sweeney chuckled.

"O.K.," said Les, "I made a promise. But for now, gang, where to? We don't want to have to drive too far."

"How about the Playboy Club Hotel?" Jojo volunteered. "It's not far from here."

"Jojo the girl-watcher," laughed Sarilee.

"You mean sex maniac," Jennifer quipped. "True to his breed."

"Not this trip, Jojo," his father replied. "Any other ideas?"

"There's always the Tower Isle," offered Millie without hesitation. "It's the closest population center."

"Dullsville," Jennifer groaned. "We've been there already."

122

"Dullsville, my eye," Millie retorted. "It's a safety valve. They'll get so used to seeing us that we'll be welcomed with open arms just in case we have to flee there in the middle of the night."

"That's it," said Les, "we're going to Dullsville."

"Hup anchor," Sweeney called out. "Let go the bow loine."

Sweeney and the Framers returned to Limeshade Villa about midnight. They had spent an uneventful evening at the Tower Isle.

Jennifer, Sarilee, and Jojo had wandered aimlessly all over the hotel looking for excitement. They found none.

Les and Millie, having enjoyed a few rum punches in the quiet lobby cocktail lounge, slowly strolled around the lush grounds of the hotel. They finally settled down on the promenade fronting the glistening, moonlit Caribbean Sea. They spoke little, made content, if not altogether serene, by the twinkling heavens above and the gentle movement of the water ahead.

Sweeney, too, found a place for himself—on the beach. There, alone, in that tranquil tropical space with the hotel at his back and the timeless sea at his feet, he sat and wistfully peered at the distant horizon, dreaming his dreams of long ago.

SATURDAY
February 26, 1972

The milling throng gaped and froze as Les turned the corner on two wheels and brought the car to a screeching halt in front of the departure wing of the airport terminal.

The calm deliberate voice on the loudspeaker announcing arrivals and departures was in pointed contrast to the frantic mob of Framers that tumbled from the car.

"Everyone out," ordered Les, keeping the engine running. "We've got forty-five minutes and plenty to do."

"We are out!" screamed Millie. "God, it's hot. What next?"

125

"You pay the exit tax, honey. The kids'll get us a place at the Pan Am counter—with baggage—so we can get ourselves checked in—they'll need the paid tax receipts to do that. I'll get rid of the car and meet you at the counter. See if you can get us all sitting together. By."

"Wait!" Millie screamed as Les gunned the motor. "You can't go yet! Our luggage is in the trunk and you have all the tickets!"

Les vaulted from the car like a kangaroo, shoved the tickets at Millie, opened the trunk of the car and began hauling everything out. A porter came along and Les, soaked with perspiration, turned the hauling over to him.

"Now we've got forty minutes left!"

"Whose fault is that? We left in plenty of time but you had to go and get a flat."

"Listen! We had a quiet night. Right? Right. Sweeney left us alone. Right? Right. He finished with us and now we are finished with him. Right? Right. In thirty-eight minutes at exactly two forty-five we had better be aboard Pan Am 222 or Sweeney may find us again. Right? Right. So let's get with it."

Les roared off and disappeared into the traffic. Millie found the tax man. Jennifer, Sarilee, and Jojo followed the porter with their luggage to the Pan Am counter and got in line.

Les turned up fifteen minutes later, wheezing from lack of breath.

126

"I can't run any more," he complained. "Everything taken care of at this end?" Now that home and business was once more within reach, Les was beginning to sound like the executive he had left behind in the New York snow last week. "We've got twenty-three minutes and they are probably boarding now."

"All set."

"Let's go."

"You didn't forget that stuff you bought, did you, Dad?" asked Sarilee.

"No. And time may have run out. We have to get past immigration again and pass into the waiting room. The duty-free place that has our order is in there."

The waiting room was hot, sticky, and jammed with a mass of people that was beyond description. The Framers located their boarding gate and found that nearly four hundred of those people belonged to their flight. No one, as yet, had been permitted to board the giant jet.

"I wonder what's going on?" Les thought out loud.

A moment later several uniformed Pan Am officials circulated through the crowd announcing that Flight 222 would be delayed about an hour. They tried to make the announcement over the loudspeakers earlier but nobody could understand what they were talking about.

"Great!" Les declared. "Now we can pick up the liqueur. Come on, Jojo. We've got some time. Let's go over there and see if they have our package."

Like elsewhere in the waiting room, the duty-free counter was packed solid. Buying things at cost—tax free, provided the items purchased were not used on Jamaican soil—was a luxury that no Jamaican could enjoy. Only visitors to the island had that privilege. In this way, for example, an American vacationer could buy things at half the price they would cost at home.

"I wonder what happened, Dad?"

128

"Wish I knew, Jojo. It's probably nothing. Maybe the captain wants something checked out. Usually that takes time."

"Are you talking about Pan Am 222?" asked a burly, sweaty stranger behind them.

"Yes."

"Darndest thing I ever heard of," he said. "Someone pushed the wrong button and all the oxygen masks fell out of their overhead cupboards—about four hundred of them."

"Why should that delay the flight for an hour?"

"Maybe longer," the man continued. "Every one of those masks has to be replaced correctly by hand."

"Whew," said Les as he handed over his sales receipt and picked up the package of liqueur.

"Sweeney," Jojo whispered to his father.

"Nonsense."

"Sweeney's here," Jojo insisted.

"*That's right, Governor. The lad knows. Hits me all right. Oi'm 'ere. Sweeney 'imself. Now Oi couldn't let ye go without a proper farewell. Hit wouldn't be fitting.*"

"Don't think it. Don't mention it, Jojo," his father warned. "I think you're being silly. Just the same let's not drive your mother up the wall."

Les and Jojo joined Millie and the girls near the boarding gate.

"Guess who we saw a few minutes ago?" Sarilee asked her brother and father. She then went on to answer her own question. "That sword swallower and his daughter. And you're not going to believe this. Remember the crazy act he put on? Remember how he was dragged off the stage stiff as a board? Some act, no? Funny. Right? Well, he was still stiff as a board—in a wheel chair—wrapped in a blanket— can you imagine—in this heat. Boy, was he glassy-eyed! What do you make of that?"

No one bothered to answer. Instead, once again, Les began to complain about the lack of air conditioning.

"Don't start that again, Les," Millie cautioned, "or else we'll never get out of here. Or do we have to remind you about last Saturday?"

"Now departing for JFK, New York," announced the anonymous voice over the loudspeakers, "Pan American Flight 222, Gate 3. Last call. Flight 222, Pan American. Now departing Gate 3. All aboard. Please."

The Framers found their assigned seats on the 747 toward the rear of the cool aircraft. Millie had no difficulty in having the man at the ticket counter keep them all together.

130

Unlike a week ago, the now well-tanned passengers were not quite so anxious to leave. They had to face the snow and ice they had left behind. The recording of soft, romantic music that wafted through their economy-class compartment on the trip down did little to ease the melancholy of the departure for many on board. The Framers had mixed feelings about ever returning and quietly wondered whether or not they had really been confronted by a Jamaican ghost.

The doors slammed shut. The great airplane began to whine and shudder as each of the four huge jet engines came alive. The cheerful stewardesses skipped up and down the aisles making sure that everyone was properly seated; that seat belts were fastened; that the NO SMOKING sign was being observed; and that all loose articles were safely stowed away for the take-off.

Now the big jet began to move and taxied to its flight position on the runway. There it stood, throbbing, poised, ready to fly.

"Ladies and Gentlemen, this is Captain Mathews. I should like to welcome you aboard Pan Am's Flight 222 to New York City. We apologize for the unavoidable delay and thank you for your patience. We experienced a minor annoyance which in no way impaired this aircraft's ability to perform with absolute safety. We do anticipate a smooth flight, estimating our time of arrival to be seven thirty-five Eastern Standard Time. The weather in New York is clear —temperature in the low twenty's. Our cruising altitude will be 33,000 feet; ground speed roughly 650 miles per hour. We are presently waiting for clearance—shouldn't be more than about ten minutes. Please observe the NO SMOKING and SEAT BELT indicators. While relaxing you might also observe our stewardesses demonstrate the on board safety devices. Again, our apologies for the delay. Pleasant trip."

Jojo drew his seat belt a bit tighter around his middle and looked at the vacant seat on his right. He wondered if anyone had missed the plane.

"I think this is the only empty seat back here," he said to his father as the unmistakable click of the safety belt buckle next to him reached his ear.

"That aisle seat is probably reserved for one of the steward-esses. They've got to have places to park when this thing takes off."

132

Jojo, startled, did not hear his father's explanation. He stared at the empty seat and the buckled belt. It had been unfastened a few seconds ago. Now it was fastened. And no one that he saw—not a stewardess, not a passenger, certainly not himself—had reached down and fastened it.

"Sweeney," he gasped as the engines roared and the airplane rolled down the runway with thunderous power and speed. "And he's practically in my lap!"

"Aye, laddie. Sweeney. Oi made hup me moind hat the last minute, Oi did. 'Ere was me chance to floi loike a bird. Oi couldn't resist. Oi'm going to be loike a ruddy angel! Cooooo. Won't yer mum be 'appy to 'ave me visit?"

The 747 quickly lifted into the air, gracefully arcing northeast across the sparkling Caribbean. Slowly, the great airplane straightened its flight path. It rose higher and higher until it disappeared into the Cuban sky.

LEONARD EVERETT FISHER, painter, illustrator, author, and educator, was born and raised in New York City. His formal art training began at the Heckscher Foundation in 1932 and was completed, after his wartime military service, at the Yale School of Art and Architecture, from which he received a Master of Fine Arts degree and the Winchester Fellowship. He had studied previously with Moses Soyer, Reginald Marsh, Olindo Ricci, and Serge Chermayeff. In 1950, Mr. Fisher received a Pulitzer Art Fellowship. He spent much of that year in Europe, returning home in 1951 to become dean of the Whitney School of Art in New Haven, Connecticut. He resigned from that post in 1953 and turned his attention to children's literature. Since then he has illustrated approximately two hundred children's books, about twenty-five of which he has written, including *The Death of Evening Star* and *The Warlock of Westfall*. He has received numerous citations, and in 1968 he was awarded the Premio Grafico for juvenile illustration by the International Book Fair, Bologna, Italy—the only American thus honored. Books containing his illustrations have been published in a variety of foreign languages and distributed throughout the world by the United States Information Agency. Mr. and Mrs. Fisher and their three children live in Westport, Connecticut.

DATE DUE

FEB 1 9 1982			
OCT 4 1990 NOV 2 9 87			
NOV 1 1 '94			
	DISCARDED		